An Offer He Couldn't Refuse

Remo was silent as Smith had his say. "On behalf of the organization and the American people it serves, we are grateful to you, Chiun, Master of Sinanju. And you, Remo, you will receive a large stipend every year for the rest of your life. You will remain in retirement. You may die in bed of old age, knowing you have served your country well."

"I don't believe you," said Remo. "I believe I'll get the first check and maybe the second and then one day I'll open the door and the steps will blow up in my face. *That's what I believe!*"

"I'll tell you what *I'm* offering, Smitty," Remo said. "I'm leaving. If you don't try to kill me, I won't kill you. But if by chance someone within five feet of me is poisoned or a taxi runs out of control on a street that I'm walking on or if a random shot is fired somewhere near me during a holdup, I am going to tell the world about an organization called CURE, that tried to make government work outside the Constitution. And how nothing got better and everything got worse. And then I'm going to squeeze your lemon lips into your lemon heart and we'll be even."

It was an offer Smith couldn't refuse . . .

THE DESTROYER SERIES:

The Destroyer

MUGGER BLOOD #30

by Richard Sapir & Warren Murphy

PINNACLE BOOKS   LOS ANGELES

DESTROYER #30: MUGGER BLOOD

Copyright © 1977 by Richard Sapir and Warren Murphy

An original Pinnacle Books edition published for the first time anywhere.

ISBN: 0-523-40110-8

First printing, September 1977
Second printing, December 1977
Third printing, April 1978
Fourth printing, September 1978
Fifth printing, June 1979

Cover illustration by Hector Garrido

Printed in the United States of America

PINNACLE BOOKS, INC.
2029 Century Park East
Los Angeles, California 90067

For Marolyn who is beautiful, gracious, literate, charming, intelligent, strong and a precious, precious friend.

Mugger Blood

Chapter One

At first she thought she was back in Nazi Germany. A ringing black starshine of pain was at her left eye where the boy had stuck the ice pick. She could not see left anymore. She remembered the Gestapo. But this could not be the Gestapo. The Gestapo had clean fingernails and asked clear questions and let you know that if you told them what they wanted, they would stop the pain.

The Gestapo wanted to know where Gerd was and she did not know where Gerd was. She kept saying it. But these tormenters kept saying "tawk Murican." They meant talk American.

They smelled different, these boys. You could smell them. She had told this to Mrs. Rosenbloom at the high school auditorium where the New York City Police Department had sent over someone for a morning talk. It was safe sometimes in the morning.

The police, who thought they should get more money from a near-bankrupt city, were now teaching the elderly how to get mugged. You didn't resist, they told you. You gave up your purse. There was a police lieutenant showing how to loosely fasten the straps so that the mugger would not think you were trying to hold onto your purse.

"I can smell them too," Mrs. Rosenbloom had said that morning. But she cautioned Mrs. Mueller not to mention anything. "They'll say that's racist and it is bad. You're not allowed to be racist in this country."

Mrs. Mueller nodded. She did not want to be a racist because that was a bad thing. The Nazis were that way and they were bad. She had seen what they had done and as a good Christian she could not support them. Nor could her husband Gerd.

They had wanted to reach Gerd. But Gerd was dead. A long time ago, Gerd was dead. Mrs. Mueller felt a kick in her chest. The Nazis were gone. These were blacks.

She wanted to beg the black boys not to kick her anymore. Not in the breasts. Was that what was taught in the auditorium by the New York City police? She tried to remember. Her hands were tied behind her with the electric cord. No. The police did not tell you what to do when they tied you up and put out your eye with an ice pick.

The New York City police told you how to get mugged. They never gave old people lectures on how to get killed. Maybe if they got more money, they would teach you how to be murdered as well as mugged. Mrs. Mueller thought these things in a pain-crazed mind that blended Nazi Germany and her slum apartment.

She wanted to tell the laughing black boys to kick her somewhere else. Not in the breasts because that hurt too much. Would it be racist to ask blacks to kick you somewhere else? She did not want to be a racist. She saw what racism had done.

2

But Jews never beat her up. You never had to fear for ur life in a Jewish neighborhood. This had been a wish neighborhood when she and Gerd had moved in. hey were German and thought there might be some uble because of what the Nazis had done. There was trouble. There was no trouble with the Irish who d lived two blocks over. Or the Poles. Or the Italians the other side of the Grand Concourse.

But then a law was passed. And the law said it was bad keep people out of neighborhoods. Black people. And eryone was to be taught to do the right thing. This s America. Everyone had to do the right thing.

A woman had come to talk. She taught at a univer-y. She had told everyone in the community center out George Washington Carver, a black man, and all e other nice black people and how good blacks were d how bad people who hated them were and it was a d thing to hate blacks. Gerd, who was alive then, had nslated for Mrs. Mueller. He was so smart. He knew much and learned so quickly. He had been an en-neer. If he were alive, maybe he could make the boys derstand not to kick her in the breasts but somewhere e. No, they didn't want anything. They were just ving fun with her old body.

The woman who had told everyone how nice blacks re, was the woman from the university. It was a pro-essive and good thing to welcome blacks to the neigh-rhood. The whites and blacks were all going to be lturally enriched. When the blacks started moving in d you could not walk the streets at night anymore, the ople from the university who said how nice it was to e with blacks did not come around. At first, they did t come around at night. Then when more blacks ved in, they did not come around during the day ei-er. They went off somewhere else, Gerd said, to tell her people how nice it was to live with blacks.

3

They never came to Walton Avenue anymore to te
people how culturally enriched they were to have blac
around them because now it was almost all blacks.

The ones who had money could run. But Gerd d
not have enough money anymore and they did not wa
to bother their daughter who had come to them late
life. Born in America she was. So pretty. She cou
speak English so well. Maybe she could ask these bo
not to kick her mother in the breasts where it hurt
much. Would that be racist? She didn't want to be
racist. That was a bad thing. But she didn't want to
kicked in the breasts.

She wished the black policeman were here. He wou
make them stop. There were nice blacks. But you we
not allowed to say there were nice blacks, because th
would mean there were blacks who weren't nice. An
that would be racist.

It used to be such a nice neighborhood where yo
could walk out in the street. Now you trembled whe
you had to walk past a window that was not boarde
up.

She felt the warm blood of her ripped breast con
down her belly and she tasted the blood come up h
throat and she moaned and heard them laugh at h
frail struggle to live. She felt as if her back had nails
it. Time had passed. There was no one kicking or sta
bing her anymore and that meant they might be gone.

But what did they want? They must have gotten
but there was nothing left in the apartment to ste
There wasn't even a television set any more. Yo
couldn't keep a television set because they would fii
out and steal it. No white person in the neighborhood
there were three left—had televisions anymore.

Maybe they had stolen Gerd's silly machine that
had brought with him from Germany. Maybe that w
it. What else could they have come for? They said *He*

4

Hitler a lot, these young black boys. They must have thought she was Jewish. Blacks liked to say that to Jews. Mrs. Rosenbloom said once they would come to Jewish funerals to say that and laugh.

They did not know Hitler. Hitler thought blacks were monkeys. Didn't they read? He did not think they were dangerous either, just funny monkeys.

When she was young it was her responsibility to learn how to read in school. Now that she was old, the smart people from the university who did not come around anymore said she was still responsible for other people reading. Somehow she was responsible because they could not learn to read or write.

But she could understand that. She had trouble herself learning English and Gerd always had to translate for her. Maybe these blacks spoke another language well and, like she did, they just had trouble with English. Did they speak African?

She could not feel her arms anymore and the left side of her head was numbed from pain in a faraway place and she knew she was dying, tied here to her bed. She could not see from her right eye whether it was dark yet because you had to board up your windows if you wanted to walk from room to room. Otherwise you had to crawl below the level of the windowsill so they would not see you. Mrs. Rosenbloom could remember when old people would sit in the sun in the park and young boys and girls would actually help you across a street.

But Mrs. Rosenbloom had gone in the spring. She had said she wanted to smell a fresh flower at noon again and she had remembered that before blacks had moved into the neighborhood there were daffodils in St. James Park in the spring and she was going to try to smell one in the bright sun. She knew they had to be up by now. So she had phoned and said goodbye in case something should happen. Gerd had warned her not to go but she had said she was tired of living without sunshine and even though she had the misfortune to live in a now dangerous place, she wanted to walk in the sun again. It was not her fault her skin was white and she was too poor to move away from blacks and she was too old to run or to fight them off. Maybe if she just walked out on the street, as if she had a right to, maybe she could get to the park and back.

And so Mrs. Rosenbloom had headed for the park that noon and the next day when Gerd had phoned one of the other whites who could not leave the neighborhood, he found out that Mrs. Rosenbloom had not contacted them either. Her phone did not answer.

Gerd reasoned that since there was nothing on the radio—he had a small silent earphone put in because that way you could keep a radio because they wouldn't know you had one and come to steal it—then Mrs. Rosenbloom was dead cleanly. The radio and the newspapers only had stories when they poured gasoline over you and burned you alive as in Boston or when whites committed suicide because the fear of blacks was too great as in Manhattan. The normal everyday deaths were not on the radio, so perhaps Mrs. Rosenbloom had died quickly and easily.

And later they saw someone who had known someone who had seen her body picked up, so she was dead definitely. It was not a wise move to go to the park. She should have waited for the New York City police to give a lecture on how to be mugged in the park, or gone in the very early hours when the only blacks out were the ones who worked and they left you alone. But she had wanted to smell the flowers under the noonday sun. There were worse things to die for than to smell a daffodil in the full sun. Mrs. Rosenbloom must have died cleanly. That was good in a neighborhood like this.

Was it a month ago that Mrs. Rosenbloom died? Two

6

onths? No, it was last year. When did Gerd die? When
id they leave Germany? This was not Germany. No.
his was America. And she was dying. It felt all right as
this was the way it should be. She wanted to die to go
to that night where her husband waited. She knew she
ould see him again and was glad he had not lived to
bserve how horribly she was dying because she could
ever explain to him that it was all right. That it
oked worse than it was and already, Gerd darling, she
uld feel the senses of the body leave, there being no
ore need for pain when the body dies.

And she gave God her last thanks on earth and felt
od leaving her body.

When the life went from the frail old whitened form
d the heat went and the blood stopped moving in the
ins, the ninety-two pounds of human flesh that had
en Mrs. Gerd Mueller did what flesh always did unless
ozen or dried. It decomposed. And it smelled so fright-
lly that the New York City police finally came to col-
ct it. Two large men with unholstered guns provided
otection for the coroner's office. They made comments
out the neighborhood and when the body was leaving
the stretcher, a gang of black youths cornered one of
e policemen who fired off a shot, catching underarm
sh from one of the young men. The gang fled and the
dy went to the morgue untroubled and the detectives
ed their reports and went home to the suburbs where
ey could raise their families sanely, in relative safety.

A boozy old reporter who had once worked for the
any newspapers in New York City and now worked for
television station leafed through the homicide reports.
was just another old white person killed by blacks and
put it back in a pile of such reports. It offended him
at human life would be so insignificant now, as if the
y were at war. And it reminded him of another time,
en deaths were also unimportant. It was thirty years

7

before when blacks shooting other blacks just was no news.

He put down the reports and answered a call from the newsroom. A detective in the Bronx, trapped by gang of black youths, had fired and wounded one. The Black Ministry Council of Greater New York was calling the shooting "barbarism." They were picketing the house of the policeman's lawyer, demanding an end to legal defense of policemen accused of shooting blacks.

The reporter was told by his assignment editor to line up with a camera and do an interview in front of the lawyer's home.

The pickets were lounging in cars when the reporter got there. He had to wait for his cameraman. When the camera arrived, it was as if everyone had suddenly been injected with adrenalin. Out of cars and off car hoods they came. They joined the circle and the cameraman got precisely the right angle to make it look as if an entire community was marching in front of this lawyer's house.

They chanted and marched. The reporter put the microphone in front of a very black man with a very white collar under his rutted face.

The reverend talked of maniacal policemen shooting down innocent black youths, the victims of "the worst racism ever seen by man."

The black man identified himself as Reverend Josiah Wadson, chairman of the Black Ministry Council, cochairman of the World Church Group, executive director of Affirmative Housing Action I, soon to be followed by Affirmative Housing Action II. His voice rolled like mountains in Tennessee. He invoked the righteous wrath of the Almighty. He bemoaned white barbarism.

The reporter wished fervently that Reverend Wadson

8

a massive man, would talk upward instead of downward at the reporter, and, if possible, hold his breath.

Reverend Wadson reeked gin and his breath could have peeled epoxy off a battleship turret. The reporter tried to hide how painful it was to stand near Reverend Wadson's breath.

Wadson called for an end to police brutality against blacks. He talked of oppression. The reporter tried to hold his own breath so he would not have to inhale so close to the reverend.

He also had to hide the bulge under the reverend's black mohair jacket. The reverend packed a pearl-handled revolver and the assignment editor would never allow this film to appear showing that the reverend went around armed. The assignment editor didn't want to appear racist; therefore all blacks had to appear good. And unarmed, of course.

When the film appeared and was grabbed up by the network, there was the sonorous weeping voice of the reverend describing the awful plight of black youths and there were the outraged citizenry behind him, marching in protest, and there was the reporter hunched up, blocking the view of the reverend's gun, and the reporter was turning away every so often and when his face came back close to the reverend's, there were tears in his eyes. It looked as if the story the reverend told was so sad that the veteran reporter could not refrain from sobbing on camera.

When it was showed overseas, this was just what the foreign news announcers said. So terrible was the police oppression of black youths that a hardened white reporter broke down in tears. This little news clip became famous within days.

Professors sat around discussing police brutality, which became oppression, which became naturally enough "New York City police-planned genocide."

When someone brought up the incredibly high crime rate of blacks, the learned response was what could one expect after such attempted police genocide? It was asked on tests in universities. And those who did not know this answer failed.

Meanwhile, Mrs. Gerd Mueller was buried with a closed casket. The funeral home had attempted to resurrect the left side of the old face but the wax rebuilding where her eye had been proved too difficult with old flesh. They couldn't turn in the folds in wax to build up her old cheek. It looked too young for the immigrant from Germany.

So they shielded everyone's eyes from what the muggers had done, and when the casket was brought from the church to Our Lady of Angels cemetery there was a large cortege. And this surprised Mrs. Mueller's daughter because she did not know that her parents knew that many people, especially men in their thirties and forties. And a few of them who asked questions.

No, her parents had left nothing. Oh, there was a safe deposit box that held only a few bonds. Trinkets. That's what one mourner said he was looking for. Trinkets. Old German trinkets.

And the daughter thought this was shocking. But what was really shocking in today's world? So a buyer wanted to do business at graveside? Maybe that was his thing? And she longed for the days when some things had been shocking, because her heart hurt fiercely and she thought of the old woman dying alone and how frightening it had been to visit her parents after the neighborhood had changed.

"No bloody trinkets, damn you," she yelled.

And that day, wreckers began taking down the apartment building where the Muellers had lived.

They moved in with an armed escort of federal marshals, each over six feet tall and karate trained. They sealed off the street. They built armor-plated barricades. They carried truncheons. The old walk-up building was taken down with surgical precision brick by brick, and the debris left the area, not by truckloads, but in large white trunks. With padlocks.

Chapter Two

His name was Remo and he was taking the elevator up—
from beneath. He smelled the heavy buildup of engine
fumes embedded in the caked grease, and felt long
cables tremble ever so slightly when the elevator came to
a floor and that fifteen-story ripple started with a halt of
the elevator and shimmied down to the basement and
then back up past the fifteenth floor to the penthouse,
five stories overhead.

He had a good forearm hold on a bolt that he kept
just above his lean frame. People who held onto things
for their lives usually tired quickly, precisely because
they held on for their lives. Fear gave speed and power
to the muscles, not endurance.

If one wanted to hold onto something, one became a
solid part of it, extended himself out through the ex-
truding bolt, so that the grip did not strangle but extended from what it was joined to. As he had been
taught, he let the hand do the attaching lightly and for-

12

got about it. So that when the elevator started again, his body swayed easily from the hand that was the pivot joint and up he went.

It was his right hand and he could hear people walking just above his right ear.

He had been there since early morning and when the elevator stopped at the penthouse floor, he knew he would not be there much longer. At the penthouse floor, different things happened. Remo heard locks snap, twenty stories down, twenty locks, each for an elevator door. He had been told about this. He heard the grunt of muscled men who forced themselves up through strain. They checked the top of the elevator. He had been told about that also. The bodyguards always checked the roof of the elevator because it was known men could hide there.

The roof was sealed with reinforced steel plating and so was the floor. This prevented anyone from burrowing down or up into the elevator.

The elevator to the street was the only vulnerable point in the penthouse complex of the South Korean consul in Los Angeles. The rest was a fortress. Remo had been told about that.

And when he was asked how he would penetrate this complex, he answered that he was paid for his services, not his wisdom. Which was true. But even truer was that Remo did not really know how he was going to penetrate this complex at the time and he didn't feel like thinking about it, and most of all, he hadn't felt like carrying on the conversation. So he threw out some wiseacre comment, the kind he himself had endured for more than a decade, and on the morning that upstairs wanted the job done, he sauntered over to the building with the elegant penthouse fortress and made his first move without even thinking.

One did not have to scheme too much anymore. At

13

first, the defenses he had run into—where people locked gates or lived high up or surrounded themselves with bodyguards—had presented problems. And it was very exciting at first to solve them.

This morning, for some reason, he had been thinking about daffodils. He had seen some earlier in the spring and this morning he was thinking about these yellow flowers and how now when he smelled them, it was entirely different from the way he had smelled them before, before he had become this other person he now was. In the old days, there might have been a sweet odor. But now when he smelled a flower, he could inhale its movements. It was a symphony of pollen climaxing in his nostrils. It was a chorus and a shout of life. To be Sinanju, to be a learner and a knower of the disciplines of the small North Korean village on the West Korean Bay, was to know life more fully. A second now had more life in it than an hour had had before.

Of course, sometimes Remo didn't want more life. He would have preferred less of it.

So, thinking of these yellow flowers, he entered the new white brick-and-aluminum building with the full story-high windows and the elegant marble entranceway and the waterfall going over the plastic flowers in the lobby, took the elevator up to the tenth floor. There, he fiddled around with the stop and emergency buttons until he got the tenth floor about waist-high, then slid under the elevator, found a bolt on the undercarriage, locked his right hand to it, until amid screaming from many floors, someone got the elevator started again. And there he waited and swung until later when the elevator went all the way up to the penthouse.

Not much thinking. He had been told so early by his teacher, by Chiun, current Master of Sinanju, that people always show you the best way to attack them.

If they have a weakness, they surround it with ditches

14

or armor plating or bodyguards. So Remo, upon hearing of all the protection around the elevator when he got the assignment, went right to the elevator, thinking of daffodils because there wasn't really much else to think about.

And now, the person he wanted walked into the elevator, asking questions in Korean. Were all the locks on so the trip down could not be interrupted? They were, Colonel. Was the top hatch secure? Yes, Colonel. The roof entrance? Yes, Colonel. The floor? Yes, Colonel. And, Colonel, you look so splendid in your gray suit.

Most American, no?

Yes, like a businessman.

It is all business.

Yes, Colonel.

And the twenty stories of cable moved.

And the elevator lowered.

And Remo rocked his body. The elevator descending in a long slow drop of twenty stories rocked with the light human form on its undercarriage, like a bell with a swinging clapper. It picked up the back-and-forth of the rhythm-perfect sinew machine on its undercarriage, and at the twelfth floor, the elevator began banging its guide rails, spitting sparks and shivering the inside panels.

The occupants pressed emergency stop. The coils snapped to a quivering stillness. Remo took three slow swings, and on the third, hand-ladled his body up into the floor space at the door opening above him, and then, getting his left hand up into the rubber of the inner elevator door, gave the whole sliding mechanism a good bang and a healthy shove with his left side.

The door opened like a champagne cork popping into an aluminum cradle. And Remo was inside the elevator.

"Hello," he said in his most polite Korean but he knew, even with his heavy American accent, the tones of

15

the greeting were sodden with the heaviness of the northern Korean town of Sinanju, the only accent Remo had ever learned.

The short Korean with the lean hard face had a .38 Police Special out of the shoulder holster under his blue jacket with good speed. It told Remo that the man in the gray was definitely the colonel and the one he wanted. Koreans, when they had bodyguards, thought it beneath their dignity to fight. And this was somewhat strange because the colonel was supposed to be one of the most deadly men in the south of that country with both hand and knife, and, if he wished, the gun too.

"I don't suppose that would pose any problem to you?" Remo had been asked when given the assignment and told of the colonel's skills.

"Nah," Remo had said.

"He has the renowned black belt in karate," Remo had been told.

"Yeah, hmmm," Remo had said, not all that interested.

"Would you like to see his moves in action then?"

"Nah," Remo had said.

"He is perhaps one of the most feared men in Asia. He is very close to South Korea's president. We need him alive. He's a fanatic so that may not be easy." This warning had come from Dr. Harold W. Smith, director of Folcroft Sanitarium, the cover for a special organization which worked outside the laws of the land, in the hope that the rest of the system could work inside. Remo was its silent enforcement arm and Chiun the teacher who had given him more than American money could buy.

For while the assassins of Sinanju had rented out their services to emperors and kings and pharaohs even before the Western world started keeping track of years by numbers, they never sold how they did it.

16

So when the organization paid for Chiun to teach Remo to kill, they got their money's worth. But when Chiun taught Remo to breathe and live and think and explore the inner universe of his own body, creating a creature that used its brain cells and body organs at least eight times more effectively than normal man, Chiun gave the secret organization more than it had bargained for. A new man, totally different from the one sent to him for training.

And Remo could not explain it. He could not tell Smith what the teachings of Sinanju had given him. It would be like trying to explain soft to someone who could not feel or red to a person born blind. You did not explain Sinanju and what the masters knew and taught to someone who was going to ask you someday if you might have trouble with a karate expert. Does the winter have trouble with the snow? Someone who thought of Remo's watching movies of another fighter in action could not possibly understand Sinanju. Ever.

But Smith had insisted upon showing the movies of the colonel in action. It was taken by the CIA which had worked heavily with the colonel at one time. Now there was a strain between Korea and America and the colonel was one of the larger parts of it. They could not get to him because he had become familiar with American weapons. It was like a teacher trying to trick an old pupil who had grown too wise. It was just the sort of mission Smith thought the organization would be good for.

"That's nice," Remo had said and whistled an off-key tune in the hotel room in Denver where he had gotten the assignment for the Korean colonel. Smith, undeterred by Remo's indifference that had blossomed into yawning boredom, ran the movies of the colonel in action. The colonel broke a few boards, kicked a few

17

younger men in the jaw, and danced around a bit. The movie was black and white.

"Whew," Smith had said. He arched an eyebrow, a very severe emotion on that normally frosted face.

"Yeah, wha'?" asked Remo. What was Smith talking about?

"I couldn't see his hands," said Smith.

"Not that fast," said Remo. After awhile you had to listen and observe people to find out where their limits were, because sometimes you just couldn't believe how dead they were to life. Smith really believed the man was fast and dangerous, Remo realized.

"His hands were a blur," said Smith.

"Nah," said Remo. "Stop the frames where he's flailing around. They're sharp."

"You mean to tell me you can see individual frames in a movie?" asked Smith. "That's impossible."

"As a matter of fact, unless I remind myself to relax, that's all I see. It's all a bunch of stills."

"You couldn't see his hands in still frames," Smith challenged.

"All right, fine," said Remo pleasantly. If Smith wanted to believe that, fine. Was there anything else that Smith wanted.

Smith dimmed the lights in the hotel room and put the small movie projector into reverse. The lights flickered into a blur, as the camera whirred and then stopped. There was the still frame. And there was the colonel's striking hand, frozen and clear. Smith moved the camera still by still to another frame, then another. The hand was picture-sharp throughout, not too fast for the film at all.

"But it looked so fast," said Smith. So regularly and consistently had he acknowledged that Remo had changed that he was not aware of how much had truly happened, how much Remo had really changed.

18

And Remo told him more that he thought had changed. "When I first started doing all this for you, I used to respect what we were doing. No more," Remo had said, and he had left that hotel room with instructions on what America wanted from the Korean colonel. He could have had a few hours' briefing on how the CIA and the FBI had failed to reach the man, what his defenses were, but all he wanted was a general description of the building so he could find it. And, of course, Smitty had mentioned the protection on the elevator.

So Remo watched the .38 Special come around toward him from the man in the blue suit and watched the man in the gray suit back away to let his servant do the job and that was good enough identification for him.

He caught the gun wrist with a forefinger, snapping it through the bone. He did this in such perfect consonance with the bodyguard's own rhythm, it appeared as if the man had taken the gun out of the holster only to throw it away. The hand didn't stop moving and the gun flew into the open crack between floors and down into silence. As Remo cupped his hand behind the head, he gave his fingers and palms an extra little twist. This was not a stroke he had been taught. He wanted to wipe away the grease from the elevator's undercarriage. He did that as he brought the guard's head down into his rising knee—one, pushing through with a tidy snap at the end, right behind the man's head toward the open wall; two, caught the returning body; and three, put it to rest quietly and forever on its back.

"Hi, sweetheart," said Remo to the colonel in English. "I need your cooperation." The colonel threw his briefcase at Remo's head. It hit a wall and snapped open, spilling packages of green American money. Apparently the colonel was heading to Washington to either rent or buy an American congressman.

The colonel assumed a dragon position with arching

hands like claws, and elbows forward. The colonel hissed. Remo wondered whether there were sales on American congressmen like any other commodity. Did one get the votes of a dozen congressmen cheaper than buying twelve separately? Was a vote ever reduced to a bargain? What was the price of a Supreme Court justice? And what about cabinet members? Could someone purchase something in a nice secretary of commerce?

The colonel kicked.

Or perhaps rent a director of the FBI? Could a buyer be interested in a vice president? They were really very cheap. The last one sold out for cash in an envelope, bringing disgrace to a White House already full of it. Imagine a vice president selling out for only fifty thousand dollars in cash payoff. That brought shame to his office and his country. For fifty thousand dollars, one should get no more than a vice president of Greece. It was a disgrace to be able to buy an American vice president for so little.

Remo caught the kick.

But what could one expect from anyone who would write a book for money?

The colonel threw a kick with the other leg, which Remo caught, and returned the foot to the floor. The colonel sent a stroke that could crush brick at Remo's skull. Remo caught the hand and put it back at the colonel's side. Then came the other hand, and back it went too.

Perhaps, thought Remo, American Express or Master Charge might simply credit an account, or every freshman congressman would get one of the stickers of those credit agencies and attach it to his office door and when someone wanted to bribe him, he wouldn't have to carry cash out into the dangerous Washington streets, but just present his credit card and the congressman could take out one of those machines he would get when he swore to uphold the Constitution as he took office, and run through the briber's credit card and at the end of every month get his bribe through his own bank. Just bribing a congressman with cold cash was demeaning.

The colonel bared his teeth and lunged, trying to get a bite at Remo's throat.

Possibly, thought Remo, there might even be a stock market for Washington politicians, with bids on farm votes and things like that. Senators up three points, congressmen down an eighth, the president steady. And while his thoughts were sarcastic, Remo was greatly sad. Because he did not want his government to be that, he did not want that stain of corruption, he not only wanted to believe in his country and his government, he wanted the facts to justify it also. It was not even good enough the majority were honest, he wanted all of them that way. And he hated the money strewn around this elevator floor as he throttled the Korean colonel. For that money was destined for American politicians and it meant that there were hands out.

So this little thing with the colonel was a bit of a pleasure and he leveled the man and put him on his back and very slowly he said—so that the man would be sure this was not just a windy threat—"Colonel, I am about to puree your face in my hands. You can save your face and your lungs which can be snapped out of your body and your gonads and various other parts of your body that you will miss tremendously. You can do this by cooperating. I am a busy man, Colonel."

And in Korean, the colonel gasped: "Who are you?"

"Would you believe a Freudian analyst?" asked Remo, pressing his right thumb under the colonel's cheekbone and pressing down so that the left eye of the colonel strained at its nerve endings.

"*Aieee,*" screamed the colonel.

"And so, please dig deep into your subconscious and

come up with your payroll of American politicians. All right, sweetie?" said Remo.

"*Aieeee*," screamed the colonel, because it felt as if the eye were coming out of its socket.

"Very good," said Remo and released pressure. The eye eased back into the socket, suddenly filled with a roadmap of red veins as the burst capillaries flooded the eyeball. The red lines in the left eye would disappear in two days. And by the time they did, the colonel would be a defector in the custody of the FBI. He would be called a key witness and newsmen would say he defected because he was afraid of returning to South Korea which of course made no sense for he was one of the closest friends of the South Korean president. And the colonel would name names and how much each one got.

And Remo hoped they would go to jail. It offended him that the grease-slicked head with the little rat grin of a former vice president went pandering around the world when he should have been behind bars doing time like the common thief he was.

So he told the colonel very clearly and very slowly in English and in Korean that all the names would be named and that there was nothing that could protect the colonel.

"Because, Colonel, I have greater access to your nerves and to your pain than you do," said Remo, as the elevator closed its door and descended toward the basement.

"Who are you?" asked the colonel, whose English occasionally lost verbs but who pronounced any figure above ten thousand dollars flawlessly. "You work for me. Fifty thousand dollars."

"You're not talking to a vice president of the United States," said Remo angrily.

"A hundred thousand."

"Nobody voted me into office, buddy," said Remo.

"Two hundred thousand. I make you rich. You work or me."

"You don't understand. I am not the director of the FBI. I've never sworn to uphold the Constitution and carry out any duties on behalf of the American people. I'm not for sale," said Remo and took one of the bundles of new one hundred dollar bills and put the edge of it into the colonel's mouth.

"Eat. It's good for you. Eat. Please. Just a nibble. Try it, you'll like it," said Remo, and as the colonel tried to chew at the corner of the paper, Remo told him who he was.

"I'm the spirit of America, Colonel. The man who walked on the moon, who invented the light bulb, who grows more food on his land because of his own sweat than any other. If I have a fault, it's that I've been too kind to too many people too often. Eat."

When the elevator reached the lower security area and the door opened, the guards at the door saw only their commander leaning numbly against the back of the elevator and his bodyguard stretched dead upon the floor, his right hand loose jelly in unpunctured skin. Money was strewn around the elevator floor and for some strange reason, the colonel was chewing on the end of a packet of bills.

"Take me to the FBI immediately," he said in a daze.

When they were gone, Remo slid from the undercarriage where he had waited before and squirmed his way through a breadbox-sized hole, out into the garage.

He heard people yelling all the way up the twenty stories of the building at the closed and locked elevator doors. He smiled at a startled guard.

By noon, Remo was back at the trim white yacht in San Francisco Bay that he had left early that morning.

He moved quietly because he did not wish to disturb what was happening in the cabin. It sounded like iron pans being clanged against a blackboard. Remo waited outside and noticed that the sounds went on uninterrupted. It was Chiun reciting his poetry and usually he would stop to give himself reviews, the style of which he had read in American papers.

He would normally tell himself: "Superb with the power of genius ... iridescent magnificence, defining the very role itself." The role Chiun was defining at this moment was that of the wounded flower in his 3,008-page poem that had already been rejected by twenty-two American publishers. An insensitive bee had plucked his pollen too rapidly.

The poem was in old Korean, the Korean dialect uninfluenced by Japanese. Remo peered into the cabin and saw the crimson and gold kimono of Chiun's poetry robe. He saw the long fingernails gracefully glide into the positions of a flower and then the flutter of a bee. He saw the wisps of white hair and the faint long delicate beard and realized that the deadliest assassin in the world had a visitor.

He looked farther around through the little porthole and he saw the shined black cordovan shoes on the carpet. The visitor was Dr. Harold W. Smith.

Remo let the director sit through another half hour of the Ung poetry which Smith could not possibly understand because he did not know Korean. But such was Smith's great ability to deal with government figures that he could sit appearing interested hours on end, listening to what had to be to him just discordant sounds. He could have been hearing a record of dishes being washed and gotten as much real information from it. But here he was, eyebrows curled, thin lips pursed, head cocked ever so slightly, as if he were taking notes at a college lecture.

At a pause, Remo entered amid Smith's applause.

"Did you get the significance of that, Smitty?" asked Remo.

"I'm not familiar with the form," said Smith, "but what I do understand, I appreciate."

"What do you understand?" Remo asked.

"The hand movements. They were a flower, I assume," said Smith.

Chiun nodded. "Yes. Some are uncultured dregs and others have sensitivity. Perhaps it is my special burden that I am condemned to teach those who least appreciate it. That I, to earn tribute for my village as my ancestors before me, must squander the wisdom of Sinanju before the ingrate who has just arrived. Diamonds in the mud. A pale piece of a pig's ear, here before you."

"*Barf*," said Remo, in the manner of the Americans.

"Ah, you see here the gratitude," said Chiun to Smith with a satisfied nod.

Smith leaned forward. His lemony face was even more somber than usual.

"I imagine you are wondering why I would appear here before both of you, so close to a spot where I assume you have just completed an assignment. I have never done this before, as you both know. We go to great pains to keep ourselves and our operations from public knowledge. Public knowledge of our operations would ruin us. It would be an admission that our government operates illegally."

"Oh, Emperor Smith," said Chiun. "He who holds the strongest sword makes his slightest whim legal."

Smith nodded in respect. This always amused Remo, when Smith tried to explain democracy to Chiun. For the House of Sinanju had served only kings and despots, the only ones with enough money to pay tribute to the assassins of Sinanju for the support of the village on rocky Korean coast. It did not occur to Remo at that moment that Smith was about to try to buy Chiun away from Remo, with fortunes far beyond those of petty kings and pharaohs.

"So I must be aboveboard in this," said Smith. "I have found you more and more difficult to deal with, Remo. Incredibly difficult."

Chiun smiled and his lined, aged face moved up and down in a nod. He noted that lo these many years he had endured Remo's lack of respect in gentle silence, not letting the world know what it was to give the great treasure of the knowledge of Sinanju to one who was so unworthy. Chiun compared himself, in his high squeaky voice, to the beautiful flower that his poem was about, how it was stepped on, to spring back uncomplaining with its beauty for the entire world.

"Good," said Smith. "I'd hoped you'd feel that way. I really did."

"I really don't give a ding dong," Remo said.

"In front of Emperor Smith, you say those things to a Master of Sinanju?" said Chiun. Gloom shrouded the parchment face and the Master of Sinanju lowered himself to the floor of the cabin, a delicate head rising up from a mushroom of crimson and gold robe. Underneath that kimono, Remo knew the long fingernails were woven together and the legs were crossed.

"All right," said Smith. "Gracious Master of Sinanju, you have created a marvel in Remo. You, as I, find it difficult to deal with him. I am prepared to offer you now ten times the tribute we ship to your village, if you will train others."

Chiun nodded and smiled the thin calm acceptance of a flat warm lake in summer, waiting for the night to chill. This was due the House of Sinanju, Chiun said. And more was due.

"I will increase the tribute. Twenty times what we now pay," Smith said.

"Let me tell you something, Little Father," Remo said to Chiun. "The cost of the American submarine that delivers the gold to your village is more than the gold itself. He's not giving you that much."

"Fifty times the tribute," Smith said.

"See. See my worth," Chiun said to Remo. "What are you paid, white thing? Even your own whites offer me tribute tenfold. Twentyfold. A hundredfold. And you? Who offers you anything?"

"All right," said Smith who thought his last offer had been a fifty-times increase. "A hundredfold increase of eighteen-karat gold. That sort of gold is . . ."

"He knows, he knows," said Remo. "Give him a diamond and he can tell a flaw by holding it. He's a frigging jewelry store. He knows half the big stones in the world by heart. Telling Chiun about gold is like explaining the mass to the Pope."

"To support my poor village, I have become familiar to a degree with the value of things," Chiun said modestly.

"Ask him what a blue-white diamond, two karat flawless, sells for in Antwerp," said Remo to Smith. "Go ahead. Ask him."

"On behalf of the organization and the American people it serves, we are grateful to you, Chiun, Master of Sinanju. And you, Remo, you will receive a large stipend every year for the rest of your life. You will remain in retirement. You may die in bed of old age, knowing you have served your country well."

"I don't believe you," said Remo. "I believe I'll get the first check and maybe the second and then one day I'll open the door and the steps will blow up in my face. That's what I believe."

Remo loomed over Smith and let his left hand float under Smith's chin so Smith would realize Remo was willing to kill with that hand right now. He wanted his body presence to dominate Smith. But the stern man was not about to be dominated by a threat. His voice did not waver as he repeated the offer to the man who had taken the organization so far by himself. In Remo, the organization had the ultimate killer arm, the human being maximized to its highest potential. How Chiun had gotten this from Remo, Smith did not know. But if he could do it with one, he could do with others.

"I'll tell you what I'm offering, Smitty," Remo said. "I'm leaving. And if you don't try to kill me, I won't kill you. But if by chance someone within five feet of me is poisoned or a taxi runs out of control on a street that I'm walking on or if a random shot is fired somewhere near me during a holdup, I am going to tell the world about an organization called CURE, that tried to make government work outside the Constitution. And how nothing got better and everything got worse, except a few bodies here and there got lost. Somewhere. I don't know where. And then I'm going to squeeze your lemon lips into your lemon heart and we'll be even. So goodbye."

"I'm sorry you feel that way, Remo. I've known you felt that way for some time. When did it all start? If you don't mind my asking."

"When people couldn't walk the frigging streets and I'm running around after some secret somewhere. The country isn't working. A man puts in forty hours a week to hear some son of a bitch tell him he's got no right to eat meat, but he's got to take the food off his table and give it to people who hang around all day and call him names. Enough. And that son of a bitch who tells him that, chances are, is on some public payroll somewhere

28

making a thousand dollars a week saying how rotten this country is. No more."

"All right," said Smith sadly. "Thank you for what you have done."

"You're welcome," said Remo, without any kind feeling in it. He removed himself from over Smith and when he looked back he saw perspiration glint in the noonday sun off Smith's pale brow. Good, Remo thought. Smith had tasted fear. He had just been too proud to show it.

"And now for you, Master of Sinanju," Smith said.

Chiun nodded and spoke: "We accept your gracious offer but we have unfortunately fallen into an economic peculiarity and this distresses us so much. While we would be most happy to train hundreds, thousands, we cannot afford to. We have put more than a decade of work into this," said Chiun, nodding to Remo, "and we must protect that investment, worthless as it may seem to anyone."

"Five hundred times what your village gets now," Smith said. "And that probably means two submarines to deliver it."

"You can make it a million times more," said Remo. "He's not going to train your men. He might waltz a few people around, but he's not giving them Sinanju."

"Correct," said Chiun, elated. "I will never teach another white man Sinanju because of the disgusting ingratitude of this one. Therefore, no. I will stay with this ingrate."

"But you can be free of him and richer," Smith said. "I know of the House of Sinanju. You have done business for centuries."

"Centuries upon centuries," corrected Chiun.

"And this is more money," Smith said.

"He's not leaving me," said Remo. "I'm the best he's ever had. Better than Koreans he's had. If he could have

29

found a decent Korean to take his place someday, he never would have gone to work for you."

"Is that true?" Smith asked.

"Nothing a white man says is true, except of course your gloriousness, oh Emperor."

"It's true," Remo said. "Besides he's not leaving me. He likes me."

"*Hah,*" said Chiun imperiously. "I stay to protect my investment in that unworthy white skin. That is why the Master of Sinanju stays."

Smith stared at his briefcase. Remo had never seen the human computer so thoughtful. Finally he looked up with a small tight-lipped smile.

"I guess we're stuck with each other, Remo," he said.

"Maybe," said Remo.

"You're the only one who can do what's got to be done," Smith said.

"I'll listen but I'm not promising," Remo said.

"It's all sort of sticky. We're not sure what we're looking for."

"So what else is new?" Remo asked.

Smith nodded glumly. "About a week ago, an old lady living in a poor neighborhood was tortured to death." It happened in the Bronx, and now agents from many nations were looking for an object or device that old woman must have had. The device had been brought to this country by her husband, a German refugee, who had died shortly before she did.

The sun lowered red over the Pacific ocean and still Smith talked. When he stopped, the stars were out.

And Remo said he would do the job, if he felt like it in the morning.

Smith nodded again, as he rose to his feet.

"Goodbye, Remo. Good luck," he said.

"Luck. You don't understand luck," Remo said contemptuously.

30

"And America bids respect and honor to the awesome magnificence of the Master of Sinanju," Smith said to Chiun.

"Of course," said Chiun.

Chapter Three

Colonel Speskaya believed there was no problem that did not have a rational solution. He believed wars were started by people who really lacked information. With enough information properly organized, any fool could see who would win which war and when.

Colonel Speskaya was twenty-four and ordinarily would not have received such an august rank so young in the NKVD, the Russian secret police, except that everything he did worked out so well.

He knew more than any man the basic difference between the NKVD and the American CIA. The CIA had more money and fell on its face publicly. The NKVD had less money and fouled up in private.

Speskaya knew that in a well-run organization there should be no such thing as a twenty-four-year-old colonel in peacetime, even though for the NKVD no time was peacetime. He also knew he was going to be a general soon. Still, America was stupid also and when he was called into the American section he felt no great fear.

There was undoubtedly a problem that no one wanted to take responsibility for. When he saw the field marshal's epaulettes on the man briefing him, he knew it was a big problem.

In ten minutes, he had it just about solved.

"Your problem is that you know something big is happening in America but you're not sure what and you don't want to make any great commitment until you know, correct? You are embarrassed that we come so late into this thing in America. So we will take a look at what happened to Mrs. Gerd Mueller of the Bronx, New York, and we will see why so many intelligence agencies are hovering around there and why an entire building should be torn down by the CIA and carted off in little boxes the size of trunks. Of course, I will do myself," said Colonel Speskaya.

He was blond and blue-eyed, of delicate features that hinted of the Volga Germans. He was reasonably athletic and, as some of his women said, "technically a great lover but lacks something. He provides satisfaction the way food stores provide cheese."

Colonel Vladimir Speskaya entered the United States through Canada in midspring as Anthony Spesk. He was accompanied by his bodyguard whose name was Nathan. Nathan understood English but did not speak it. He was five-feet-two and weighed one hundred twenty pounds.

Nathan overcame this deficit in size by his willingness to shoot any warm thing. Nathan would put a .38 slug in the mouth of a baby. Nathan liked seeing blood. He hated targets. Targets didn't bleed.

Nathan confided to an instructor once that if you shot right into the heart of someone, they didn't bleed nice.

Nathan gave his advice: "Get the aorta and then you've got something."

The NKVD didn't know whether to commit him to a hospital for the criminally insane or promote him. Speskaya took him as a bodyguard and let him have his gun only when the occasion arose. Nathan asked if he could at least keep the bullets. Speskaya said this was all right provided he didn't go around polishing them in public. When Nathan wore his uniform that called for a holster, Speskaya made him carry a toy pistol. He was not about to let him walk the streets of Moscow with a loaded weapon.

Nathan was dark with a ratlike face and protruding front teeth that looked as if he were a new race of man that fed on birch bark.

When Colonel Speskaya, alias Anthony Spesk, reached Seneca Falls, New York, he took a new .38 caliber pistol from his suitcase—border police never checked one's baggage between Canada and America—and gave it to Nathan.

"Nathan, this is your gun. I am giving this to you because I trust you. I trust you know how much Mother Russia depends on you. You will be able to use this gun but only when I say so. All right?"

"I swear. By all the saints and by our chairman, by the blood of all the Russians that is in me, by the heroes of Stalingrad, I swear and I pledge this caution to you, Colonel. I will, with frugality and caution, use this instrument and never without your permission will I fire even one shot."

"Good Nathan," said Anthony Spesk.

Nathan kissed his commander's hand.

At a traffic light entering the New York Thruway, Spesk felt an explosion behind his right ear. He saw a hitchhiker jump up in the air, as though being yanked

34

backward. The hitchhiker bled profusely from the chest. She had been hit in the aorta.

"Sorry," said Nathan.

"Give me the gun," said Spesk.

"I really swear this time," said Nathan.

"If you keep killing people, eventually the American police may catch us. Now come on. We have important business. Give me the gun."

"I'm sorry," said Nathan. "I said I'm sorry. I really said it. I swear it this time. I really swear it. Last time was only a promise."

"Nathan, I do not have time to argue with you. We must get away from this place because of what you have done. Do not use that gun again." Spesk let him keep the gun.

"Thank you, thank you. You are the best colonel that ever was," said Nathan, who was good all the way till New Paltz when Spesk pulled off the road to sign into a motel. Nathan shot the clerk's face off.

Spesk grabbed the gun away and drove off with the crying Nathan.

It was really not so bad as it might appear. If one studied America, as Colonel Speskaya had, one would discover that murders were rarely solved unless the murderer wanted them solved. There was just no machinery for protecting the lives of the citizens. If this were Germany or Holland, Spesk wouldn't even have brought along a bodyguard.

But America had become such a jungle that it was just not safe to enter it without protection anymore.

"I will carry the gun," said Spesk angrily as he drove off tired into the dark night heading for New York City.

"Fascist," mumbled Nathan.

"What?" demanded Spesk.

"Nothing, sir," sniffed Nathan.

It was red dawn when Colonel Speskaya entered New

York City. He told Nathan to stop making bang sounds and pointing his finger at the few people walking the streets. Nathan suddenly said he was frightened.

"Why?" asked Spesk, studying a map.

"Because we will starve to death. Or be killed in the food riots."

"You will not starve in America. Look at those shops. You can have all the food you want."

"That's only for American generals," Nathan said.

"No. It's for everyone."

"That's a lie."

"Why?" asked Spesk.

"Because Pravda says there are food riots and the people starve in America."

"Pravda is a long way away. Sometimes stories change at a distance."

"No. It's in print. I read it."

"What about American newspapers? They don't tell stories about food riots," Spesk said.

"American newspapers are propaganda."

"But they're printed too," said Spesk.

This caused Nathan some confusion. His brow furrowed. His dark Russian face clouded with gloom as he thought, difficult and sticky step by difficult and sticky step. Finally, the pistol killer smiled.

"It is Russian printing that is always the truth because you can read it right. It is American printing that lies because we cannot read it. It can say anything with those funny letters it uses."

"Good, Nathan," said Spesk, but again his bodyguard bothered him with a question so Spesk said he would explain everything about the mission now, why he had come into America personally with an operative who was not familiar with the language.

"But a good shot and a good Communist," Nathan insisted.

"Yes," said Spesk.

"So, may I have my gun?"

"No," said Spesk. "Now listen, because you are getting a rare treat," said the youngest colonel in the NKVD. "You are getting to know what is going on. Even generals don't know that."

Nathan said he knew what was going on. They were fighting imperialism. From the borders of Germany where Russian troops were stationed and into Cuba, until Russia had conquered imperialism from one end of the world to the other, where no other flag flew but the hammer and sickle.

"Good," said Spesk. "About ten days ago when you were called in from Vladivostok, a strange thing was happening in America. The CIA, our enemy, was tearing down a building piece by piece. This attracted attention. West German intelligence was interested, Argentine intelligence was interested. They did what we call overload an area and we knew that because we traced them moving large numbers of people—eight and ten, that is a lot in espionage—out of their normal duties to watch one building being torn down. To try to talk to the daughter of a woman who was killed."

"Who killed her?"

"At first we thought muggers."

"What is a mugger?" asked Nathan.

"A mugger is a person who jumps on someone, beats them up, and takes their money. There are a lot of them in New York City."

"Because of capitalist oppression, there are muggers, correct?" asked Nathan.

"No, no," said Spesk, annoyed. "I want you to understand this clearly. Forget everything you've read. In this country, there is no death penalty in many areas. Somehow they got the notion in this country that killing someone for a crime is not a deterrent to more crime. So they took away capital punishment and now they can't walk their own streets. So I have brought you along because now that this land has no death penalty, many people go around killing and you are to protect me. Worse still are the laws regarding those who are less than eighteen years old. They can kill without even going to jail and American jails are warm and give three meals a day, often with meat."

"They must have millions committing crimes to get in," said Nathan in astonishment, because only when he joined the NKVD did he eat meat regularly. That was food for ruling Communists, not for the masses.

"They have millions committing crimes," said Spesk. "But let me warn you about any idea of committing a crime to get into one of their jails. We can exchange prisoners for you and then you will go back to a Russian jail. And we kill, friend. And not all that quickly for defectors."

Nathan said he had no intention of defecting.

"Which brings up, Nathan, why I personally am here. Now you must already be thinking how stupid Americans are. And this is very true. They are stupid. If you tell Americans something is moral, they will cut their own throats for it. Except, sometimes, certain people stop them."

"Who?" demanded Nathan in the back seat of the car parked under a train that went above them on rails very high up. It was an American elevated train that some of their cities had. Every time a train passed, Nathan trembled because he thought the train might fall. Buildings fell down in Moscow so why shouldn't trains that rattled so much fall also?

"We stop them," Spesk said. "You see, our generals do not want the capitalists to cut their own throats because that would make the generals look unimportant. They want it to appear as if their hands are on the razor.

38

Therefore, they have to do something and every time they do something, they make the capitalists look smarter. Therefore, we come here to the Bronx in America. To this slum."

"It looks all right to me," said Nathan, noticing the shops open, their windows crammed with goods and foods, and how well everyone appeared to dress, without great patches, and with shoes without rags holding them on.

"By American standards it is a slum. There is worse yet, but never mind. I go here myself personally because they would, if I left it to the generals, they would write reports that said everything so no matter what happened, they would have predicted it. Our generals are as stupid as American generals. As a matter of fact, they are identical. A general is a general is a general which is why when one surrenders, he has dinner with his conqueror. They are all identical. So you and I are here to see what all this fuss is about and then we will figure out what we will do about it and when we return to Mother Russia, we will both be heroes of the Soviet Socialist Republics, yes?"

"Yes," said Nathan. "Heroes." And he thought how nice it would be to shoot up between the railroad tracks and get a kneecap or the groin. The groin was a wonderful place to shoot people except that they died only sometimes. The colonel still held his gun. But he would have to give it back when they saw muggers.

"Mugger," said Nathan happily, and pointed at a man with a blue cap and a blue suit who had a whistle in his mouth and wore white gloves and stood in the middle of a very large and wide street with high buildings all around. He would have made a wonderful target. There was even a shiny silver star on his chest. Nathan could hit that star.

"No. That is a black policeman," said Spesk. "You are thinking of nigger, not mugger. Nigger is a word Americans who are black do not like to be called."

"What do they like to be called?" asked Nathan.

"That depends. It is always changing. Once it was Negro and black was bad, then it was black and Negro was bad, then it was Afro-American, but it is never nigger. Many of the muggers are black though. Most are."

"But don't the racist police shoot black nigger Afro-Americans all the time? Negroes?"

"Obviously not," said Spesk. "Or there wouldn't be the mugging problem."

"I hate racists," said Nathan.

"Good," said Spesk. As he calculated, the building they were looking for would be toward the main center of the city which was called Manhattan, yet still in an outlying district called the Bronx.

"I also hate Africans. They are ugly and black. I want to vomit when I see something so ugly and black," Nathan said, and spat out the window. "Someday socialism will end racism and blacks."

The first thing that told Spesk they were near the area was a yellow-striped roadblock. Instead of going closer, he veered off the large American street down a hill into a residential area. If all the reports were true, anyone turning into these roadblocks passed the very casual and very armed American lounging around, would be photographed, and perhaps even stopped and questioned.

There were better ways to penetrate in America. One did not have to have expensive spies worming their way into the innards of the defense establishment. There were cheaper and easier ways. One did not have to play spy all the time in America.

So when Spesk saw the garbage stacked neatly in cans along the curb, he realized he was in a safe enough neighborhood to park. He found a tavern and told Nathan not to talk.

Spesk himself had been one of the bilingual children. Right after the Second World War, the NKVD began nurseries where children learned English and Chinese almost as soon as Russian, so that they would not only speak without accents but would think in the foreign languages also. Children, it had been discovered, learned to duplicate sounds exactly, while grownups could only reproduce sounds they had learned in their childhood. All of which meant Spesk could walk into Winarski's Tavern, just off the Grand Concourse in the Bronx of New York City, America, and sound as if he came from Chicago.

He ordered a beer, fella, and wondered, fella, how business was, fella, and gee, golly, what a great looking bar the guy had here, and by the way what were all those yellow barricades doing on the other side of the Concourse?

"Buildings. Tearing down. Niggers there," said the bartender whose English lacked Spesk's precision and clarity.

"Why are they tearing down a building, pal? Huh? How come?" asked Spesk as if he had worked his way through Douglas MacArthur High School by delivering Chicago Tribunes.

"They tear down. The politicians. They tear down, they build up."

"That's going up?"

"Nothing. Men there with guns. I bet drugs. They looking. I bet heroin," said the bartender.

"A lot of men?"

"Three blocks around. Cameras too. In apartments. You don't need to go there. Niggers over there. You stay here," said the bartender.

41

"You bet I will," said Spesk. "Say, was there anything in the papers about it? I mean, that's sort of wierd, isn't it, tearing down a building with a lot of guys with guns standing around?"

"Drugs I bet. Heroin. Does he want a drink?" asked the bartender, nodding to Nathan. Nathan stared behind the bar. Nathan drooled.

"You have a gun back there," said Spesk. "Please put it out of sight." He slapped Nathan on the shoulder and put his tongue over his lips to indicate he wanted silence.

Spesk spent the afternoon in the bar, buying drinks occasionally, playing a game of darts, and just chewing the fat with all the nice guys who came and went, fella, nice to see you, catch you again next time.

There had been a wounding of a young black there and some black minister had made a fuss, someone told Spesk. Guy's name was Wadson, Reverend Josiah. Wadson had a police record for breaking and entering, procurement, assault with a deadly weapon, rape, assault with intent to kill, even though the police had orders from City Hall to keep it quiet.

"I bet you're a cop, right?" asked Tony Spesk, alias Colonel Speskaya.

"Yeah. A sergeant," said the man.

Tony Spesk bought the guy a beer and told him the problem with New York City was that the cops' hands were tied. And they didn't get paid enough.

The sergeant thought this was true. God's honest truth. What Colonel Speskaya did not tell the sergeant was that the municipal in Moscow felt the same way, as did the London bobby and the Tanzanian people's constable.

"Wonder what all that stuff is over there? On Walton Avenue, is it?"

"Oh, that," said the sergeant. "Hush-hush. They moved the CIA in, about eight days ago. It was a fuckup."

"Yeah?" said Tony Spesk. Nathan eyed the little revolver in the sergeant's belt. He moved a hand out toward it. Spesk slapped the hand away and pushed him toward the door, motioning to their car. Spesk did not want to tell him to get out in Russian.

Back at the table, the sergeant told Spesk that he had a friend who knew one of the CIA guys there and everything was fouled up. Everything. They had been too late.

Too late for what? asked Spesk, Tony Spesk, Carbondale, Illinois appliance salesman. As with most rummies, an hour and a half of drinking had made Spesk a lifelong friend of the police sergeant. Which was how he was introduced as "my buddy, Tony" to another friend and how they all decided to go out for a night on the town because Tony had an expense account. And they took Joe with them.

Joe—you had to promise not to breathe a word of it—was an operative for the CIA.

"You're full of shit," said Tony Spesk.

"He is," said the sergeant with a wink.

They went to a Hawaiian restaurant. Joe had a Singapore Sling. He saved the little purple paper umbrellas they put in the drinks to make them cute enough to charge $3.25 for them. When Joe had collected five of those umbrellas with Tony paying, he had the damndest story to tell.

There was this German engineer. Frigging Kraut. Did he tell everybody that the guy was a German? Yeah? Okay. Well, he invented this thing, see. Whaddya mean, what thing? It was secret. Like a secret weapon. Invented it right in his Kraut cellar or attic or something.

Back during Double-U Double-U Two. Don't tell anybody because it's a secret. Now where was he?

"What kind of weapon?" asked Tony Spesk.

Joe inhaled the rummy fumes from the Singapore Sling. "Nobody knows. That's why it's a secret. I got to piss."

"Go in your pants," said Spesk with authority. The sergeant had passed out already and no one noticed that Spesk wasn't really drinking.

"All right," said Joe. "Just a minute. Okay. That takes care of that. Maybe this thing reads minds, nobody knows."

"Did you find it?" asked Spesk.

"Ooooh, it's wet," said the man earning thirty-two thousand dollars a year to protect America's interests around the world through his mental superiority, cunning, and self-discipline.

"It'll dry," said Spesk. "Did you find it?"

"It's too late," said Joe.

"Why?"

"Because I've gone already," said the agent for the most hooplaed secret service since Nero's Praetorian Guard.

"No. Why was it too late for the secret weapon?"

"It was gone. We couldn't find it. We only found out it existed because the East Germans showed up looking for it."

"And they didn't tell," said Spesk. There would be some dues to pay for this treachery toward Russia. Obviously some of the old Gestapo working now with East Germany had remembered the dead man's name and told how he had invented some kind of device, and the East German secret police went looking for it, without telling the Russian NKVD, and the Americans saw the East Germans looking and they looked, and then everybody went looking.

44

Of course, there was a possibility that America had planted something in that neighborhood to draw out spies from other countries, but Spesk dismissed that. If they caught you, they would hold you for a trade. Gone were the old Cold War illusions of being able to permanently keep other countries' operatives out of your own country.

Why bother? There was just too much traffic. They would monitor it; they wouldn't stop it. No. The story about the device was real. At least the Americans thought so. But why so much fuss? Thirty years old, the machine could not have had much practical application. Thirty years ago, there hadn't been lie detectors, biofeedback machines, sodium pentothal. A whole trip sneaking into America wasted for just a nonsense device. Spesk almost laughed. For what? To look into people's heads and see what went on? Usually it was just disconnected gibberish.

Outside, Nathan slept in the back seat of the car. American traffic was inordinately heavy outside the restaurant. No. It was normal. Spesk was judging it by Moscow standards where there were few cars. Spesk was bothered.

The CIA man, Joe, had had a night off. His operation had started only ten days before. This wasn't a night off. CIA tours went on for a minimum of twenty days and, as often as not, until a mission was completed.

Joe had a night off because the mission was over. The Americans had not found what they were looking for and they were just pulling out the CIA.

Spesk would have to look for himself.

Spesk did not often worry but tonight he was worried. He woke up Nathan and gave him his gun.

"Nathan, I am giving you the gun. Do not shoot it at anyone just yet because you will have to use it soon

45

enough. I do not want us hiding the gun because you shoot some stranger, when you may have to use it to save our lives very soon."

"Just one, now?" asked Nathan.

"None, now," said Spesk.

As he thought, he drove his large smooth American car into the area that had been sealed off by yellow painted roadblocks. The roadblocks were gone now.

It was one A.M. Black teenagers roamed the street. A few tried to break into their slow-moving car but Spesk had Nathan with him. And just showing the gun kept them away.

Spesk slowed the car at the site where the building had been torn down. He noticed a large hole in the ground. He left the car with Nathan out behind him, holding the gun. They had excavated, these Americans. They had excavated and still not found it.

Spesk's keen eyes noticed the small marks at the edge of the lot. They had excavated with chisels. Therefore the device was small. If it existed. If it was worth anything.

And then there was the shot behind him.

Nathan had done it. He had not fired to protect them. He had shot at an Oriental in glaring yellow kimono across the street and now, the white man who was with the Oriental was moving across the street.

Spesk did not have time to wonder what another white man was doing in this neighborhood. The white man moved too quickly for that. Nathan fired again and it seemed as if it was aimed right at the oncoming chest. There was no way Nathan could have missed.

And yet the thin white man was at him and virtually through him by the time the shot stopped ringing in Spesk's ear. The white man's hands hardly seemed to move, yet they were out and back and Nathan's dark skull collapsed beneath the man's fingertips and his brains went shooting out the other side as though popped from a cookie gun.

"Thank you," said Spesk. "That man was about to kill me."

Chapter Four

"Anytime I can, I'm glad to help," said Remo to the blond man, who showed an amazing coolness for someone who had moments before feared for his life. The dark-haired man with a gun lay very finally on the sidewalk, his mind not troubling him because it was spread in a fanlike pattern of brain just beyond his head like a sunrise. The slum smelled of that same strange old coffee-ground flavor Remo noticed in slums all over. They all smelled of it, even in areas that didn't use coffee. A sticky early summer coolness blew down Walton Avenue. Remo wore his usual slacks, loafers, and tee shirt.

"What's your name?" Remo asked.

"Spesk. Tony Spesk. I sell appliances."

"What were you doing out here?"

"I was driving along downtown and that man broke into my car, stuck a gun in my neck, and ordered me to drive here. I guess he decided to shoot at you when he saw you. So thanks, pal. Thanks again."

"You're welcome," Remo said. The man was over-dressed. His tie was pink. "That your car?"

"Yes," said Spesk. "Who are you? A policeman?"

"No. Not that," Remo said.

"You sound like a policeman."

"I sound like a lot of things. I sell diet gelatin. I sell strawberry and chocolate and cocoa almond cream."

"Oh," said Spesk. "That sounds interesting."

"Not as interesting as tapioca," Remo said. "Tapioca is a thrill." The man was lying of course. He had not come down to the states from Canada—the car had Canadian plates—to sell appliances. The man behind him had left the car a good time after good old Tony Spesk, to provide cover. And this was evident because the man had been more interested in roofs and windows than in the man he was supposed to be threatening.

And then the man had seen Chiun and wheeled for a shot. There was no reason for that shot. He didn't know who Chiun was, or Remo. He just shot, which was strange. But the dead dark-haired man belonged to yellow-haired Tony Spesk. There was no doubt about that.

"Do you need some help?" Remo asked.

"No, no. Do you need some help? Say, fella, I like the way you moved. You a professional athlete?"

"Sort of," Remo said.

"I can pay you double. You're not young. You're at the end of your career."

"In my game," Remo said, "young is fifty. What do you want me for?"

"I just thought a man with your abilities might want to make himself some good money, fella. That's all."

"Look," said Remo. "I really don't believe anything you've said, but I'm too busy to keep an eye on you, so just so I'll recognize you at a distance and maybe slow

49

you up a little ..." Remo let his right palm slap down at the man's knee, very gently.

And Spesk, standing there, remembered when a tank had thrown a tread and it had taken off an infantryman's knee. The calf was held to the thigh by a strand. The tank tread had shot off so fast, he had hardly seen it. This man's hand moved faster and there was a searing, emptying pain at his left knee, and even as he dropped, gasping in pain, he knew he wanted this man for Mother Russia. This man would be more valuable than any silly toy created thirty years ago. This man moved in a way Spesk had never seen before. It was not something better than any other man; it was something different.

And at twenty-four, and the youngest colonel in the Soviet, he was probably the only officer of that rank who would dare make the decision he made now, going down to the sidewalk, his left leg useless. He was going to get that man for Russia. The dunderheads in the higher ranks might not understand immediately, but eventually they would see that there was an advantage in this man, offered by no machine or device.

Spesk crawled, crying, to his car and jerkily drove away. He would find compatriots in New York who could arrange for medical care. It was not safe to lie wounded in this area, not without Nathan for protection.

Remo walked back to his car. A young black boy hopped around, clutching his wrist. Apparently he had attempted to pull Chiun's beard and had been immediately disappointed to find out here was not a frail old rabbi.

"What depths your nation has sunk to. What indescribable horrors," said Chiun.

"What's the matter?"

"That thing dared touch the body of the Master of Sinanju. Have they not been taught respect?"

"I'm surprised he's alive," Remo said.

"I have not been paid to clean the streets of your cities. Have you not had enough of this country, a country where children would dare touch the Master of Sinanju?"

"Little Father, there are things that trouble me about my country. But not fear for your person. There are other people out there though, people without your skills, who are not protected as you are by your skills. Smith is worried about some gadget that somebody invented. But I am worried because an old woman has been killed. And it doesn't matter to anyone. It doesn't matter," said Remo and he felt the blood run hot up his neck and his hands trembled and it was as if he had never been taught to breathe properly. "It's wrong. It's unjust. It goddam stinks."

Chiun smiled and looked knowingly at his pupil.

"You have learned much, Remo. You have learned to awaken your body in a world where most people's bodies go from mother's breast to grave without ever the breath of full life. Hardly is there a man to challenge your skills. Yet no master of Sinanju, for century upon century, has had skill enough to do what you wish to do."

"What is that, Little Father?"

"End injustice."

"I don't want to end it, Little Father. I just don't want it to flourish."

"Be it enough that in your own heart and your own village, justice triumphs."

And Remo knew he was about to hear the story of Sinanju again, how the village was so poor that the babies could not be supported during the lean years and had to be put to sleep in the cold waters of the West

Korea Bay. Until the first Master of Sinanju many centuries before had begun to rent out his talents to rulers. And thus was born the sun source of all the martial arts, Sinanju. And by serving well the monarchs, each Master saved the babies. This was Remo's justice.

"Each task you perform with perfection feeds the children of Sinanju," Chiun said.

"They're a bunch of ingrates in Sinanju and you know it," said Remo.

"Yes, Remo, but they are our ingrates," said Chiun, and a long fingernail stressed the point in the dark night.

It was dark because the neighborhood's street lamps had been torn down when the people discovered they could sell pieces of the new aluminum poles to junkyards. There had been a television special on the darkness in the slums, comparing it to a form of genocide, whereby the system stole light from the blacks. A sociologist made a detailed study and blamed the city for being in collusion with the junkyards to put up lights that could be torn down without too much effort. "Again, the blacks are victims," the sociologist had said on television, "of white profits." He did not dwell on who did the tearing down or whose taxes paid for the lamp posts in the first place.

Remo looked around the street. Chiun slowly shook his head.

"I'm going to find out who did in Mrs. Mueller," Remo said.

"And then what?"

"Then I am going to see that justice is done," Remo said.

"*Aieee*," wailed Chiun. "What a waste of a good assassin. My precious work and time squandered in fits of emotion." Ordinarily Chiun would seclude himself in a cloak of silence upon hearing such Western nonsense.

But this time he did not. He asked what sort of justice Remo sought. If it were youngsters who killed the old woman, then they took but a few years of her life. Should he take many years of their lives? That would be unjust.

The body of the man Remo had killed lay on the sidewalk. Police would come in the morning, thought Remo. Just as people had seen him from the windows, there must have been people who had seen the killers or killer come out of Mrs. Mueller's house. Or if it were a gang, one of them must have talked.

Smith had given Remo some details about the gadget he was looking for and about Gerd Mueller's work in Germany. The only thing mentioned about the old woman's death was that it was apparently not done by anyone important.

"You," said Remo to a fat woman leaning out the window, her large black globular breasts pushed up over her fat black arms. "You live there?"

"No. Ah just comes down here to see how the colored lives."

"I'm willing to pay for information."

"Brother," she said. She had a deep throaty voice. "That makes you down home people."

Remo offered a five and that was taken and the woman asked where the rest was. And Remo held up two hundred-dollar bills very close to her face and she made a goodly snatch at the bills, but Remo lowered them, then raised them, giving her the feeling that she had grabbed at the bills but they had dematerialized for a moment. It was so amazing to her that she tried again. And then again.

"How you do that?" asked the woman.

"I got rhythm," said Remo.

"What you wanna know?"

"There was an old woman, a white woman."

53

"De Missus Mueller."

"That's right."

"She daid. I know that the woman you want 'cause everybody axes about her."

"I know that. But do you know anyone who went into that house that day? What do you hear on the street?"

"Well, now, I been axed that a lot. And I been real fine at that. I tells them nothing. It funny they axes so much, 'cause it only a killing."

"Did you know her?"

"No. De whites don' usually go out, 'cepting 'bout de ungodly hour."

"When's that? The ungodly hour?" asked Remo.

"Nine o'clock in de morning," said the woman.

"Do you know who operates around here? What sort of gangs? Maybe they know more things. I pay good money."

"You want to know who kill her, white boy?"

"That's what I want."

"De Lawds."

"You know that?"

"Everybody know that. De Lawds, dey got dis street. It theirs. Their turf. Dey gonna get you too, white boy, lessen you come inside, you and that funny-looking yellow friend of yours."

Remo offered up the bills again and this time he let her hand close on them. But he held the bottoms of the two bills.

"How come you can lean out of that window in safety, leaving it open and all that?" Remo asked.

" 'Cause I black."

"No," said Remo. "Punks will do it to anybody weak enough. Your skin doesn't protect you."

" 'Cause I black and I blow they muthafucking heads off," she said, and with the other hand, she brought out a sawed-off shotgun. "I gots my saviour here. I got one

54

of them in the balls four years ago 'bout. He lay on that sidewalk theah and hollered. Than I gives him a bit of de ole Georgia Peach in de eyes."

"That's boiling lye?" asked Remo incredulously.

"The best. I keeps a pot boilin' all the time. Now you take you whites. They don't 'stablish themselves as peoples what got to be respected no more. I black. I speak the street language. Sawed off in the balls and lye in the face and I ain' had no trouble sincet. You and you funny-lookin' friend oughtta come in here for the night. You gonna be like that whitey you killed 'cross the street. They ain't no more white men on this block like they was yesterday. No sir."

"Thank you, granny, but I'll take my chances. The Lords, you say?"

"De Saxon Lawds."

"Thanks again."

"The policemens know about them. They knows who did it. The ones who gets the body. It was real early so I wasn't about yet but they comes out and they did that barbarous thing, over in that alley, 'cept they ain't no alley no more 'cause they takes the building down. But they was an alley then. And some boys, they up real late and they not thinkin' or nuffin' and they think it just a white folks and not a policemans and the policemans does the 'trocity, he shoots the boy in the arm. That the barbarousness of it."

Remo wasn't interested in the barbarousness of some black kid getting shot when he tried to steal a cop's gun.

"Do you know the names of the cops who know who killed the old woman?" he asked.

"Ah doan know de names of policemens. Ah doan truck wif dem. Ah doan have no numbahs, no dope."

"Thank you, ma'am, and have a pleasant evening."

"You cute there, whitey. Watch you ass, y'hear?"

The headquarters of this Bronx Police Precinct was

nicknamed Fort Mohican. Sandbags covered the windows. Remo saw a patrol car pull out of an alley with two illegal Russian Kalashnikov assault rifles and hand grenades on the dashboard.

Remo knocked on the closed precinct door.

"Come back in the morning," said a voice.

"FBI," said Remo, juggling through some identification cards he always carried. He found the FBI card with his photograph. He held it up to a small telescopic peephole in the door.

"Yeah, FBI, what do you want?"

"I want to come in and talk," said Remo. Chiun looked around with disdain.

"The mark of a civilization," Chiun said, "is how little its people need to know about defending themselves."

"Shhhh," said Remo.

"Is there someone out there with you?"

"Yes," said Remo.

"Move fifty yards away or we'll start lobbing mortars."

"I want to talk to you."

"This is a New York City police precinct. We don't open till nine A.M. for visitors."

"I'm from the FBI."

"Then tap our phones from Downtown."

"I want to talk to you."

"Did the patrol make it out safely?"

"You mean that police car?"

"Yes."

"It did."

"How did you get here at night?"

"We got here," said Remo.

"You must have had a convoy."

"No convoy. Just us."

"Look around. Is anybody loitering nearby? Anybody watching us?"

Remo turned and looked. "No," he said.

"Okay. Get in here fast." The door opened a crack and Remo eased his way in, followed by Chiun.

"What is this old guy, a magician? Is that how you got here?" asked the policeman. He had dark black hair but his face was fraught with tension and age. He kept his hand on his pistol. The officer wanted to know who Chiun was in those strange robes. He wanted to see if Chiun had a concealed weapon. He thought Chiun was a magician and that was how the two got through to Fort Mohican. His name was Sergeant Pleskoff. He had been promoted to sergeant because he had never fired at what was called "a Third World person." He knew a lot about crime. He had seen hundreds of muggings and twenty-nine homicides. And he was very close to his first arrest.

He was the new breed of American police officer, no longer a racist, hard-nosed bully but a man who could relate to his community. The other officers liked Sergeant Pleskoff too. He made sure their pay records were always in order and he wasn't one of those narrow-minded, old-fashioned annoying sort of sergeants who, when you were on duty, actually expected you to be in the state of New York.

Pleskoff kept Remo and Chiun covered with two machine guns set up on desks surrounding the front door.

Remo showed his identification.

"You probably don't know that the CIA is handling that thing on Walton Avenue," Pleskoff said.

"I'm not here about the thing on Walton Avenue. I'm here about the woman who was killed. The old woman. She was white."

"You have your nerve," said Pleskoff angrily. "You come in here and expect a New York City police precinct to be open at night, just like that, in this kind of neighborhood, and then you ask about the death of some old white lady. Which old white lady?"

"The old white lady who was tied to her bed and tortured to death."

"Which old white lady who was tied to her bed and tortured to death? You think I'm some kind of genius that remembers every white person killed in my precinct? We have computers to do that. We're not some old-fashioned police force that loses its cool just because someone gets mangled to death."

Pleskoff lit a cigarette with a gold lighter.

"Can I ask a question? I used to know a lot of cops," said Remo, "and I never used to hear talk like this. What do you do?"

"Establish a police presence in the community which relates to the needs and aspirations of the inhabitants. And, I guarantee, every officer in this precinct has been sensitized to Third World aspirations and how ... don't walk in front of the peephole so much . . . sometimes they'll come up and put a shot in the peephole. . . ."

"There's no one outside," said Remo.

"How do you know?"

"I know," said Remo.

"That's amazing. There are so many things in the world that amaze one. The other day I saw some squiggles on a piece of paper and do you know what they were made from? The human finger pads have oil on them and when you touch something, it makes a pattern, much like a linear Renoir interpretation of Sudanese sculpture. It's oval," said Pleskoff.

"It's called a fingerprint," Remo said.

"I don't read mystery fiction," Pleskoff said. "It's racist."

"I heard you people here know who killed an old white woman, Mrs. Gerd Mueller, on Walton Avenue."

"Walton Avenue, that would be either the Saxon

58

Lords or the Stone Shieks of Allah. We have a wonderful Third World program that relates to indigenous community peoples whereby we are the extension of their aspirations. We have an excellent program that teaches how the white world exploits and oppresses the black world. But we had to postpone it because of the Downstate Medical Center."

"What did they do?" asked Remo.

"With typical white insensitivity, they announced that they were buying human eyes for an eyebank. Did they realize, did they even care about the effect that would have on young indigenous Third World peoples who live here? No. They just let the word out that they would pay for eyes donated. They carelessly didn't specify that the donations should be from dead people. And we lost our program for awhile."

"I don't understand," said Remo.

"Well, the police lieutenant who gave the lecture on how the black person is always robbed by the whites, he came in here with a pair of eyes thrown right in his face by a Third World youth who had been promised so much by the Downstate Medical Center. It destroyed our good rapport with the community."

"What did?" asked Remo.

"The Medical Center ripped off the Third World again by refusing to pay for the eyes. The proud young Afro-American Third World black man, foolishly trusting the whites, brought in a pair of fresh eyes that he had obtained, and the medical center ripped him off by refusing to buy them. Said they wouldn't take a pair of fresh eyes in a Ripple bottle. Can you imagine anything so racist as that? No wonder the community is outraged."

Sergeant Pleskoff went on about the oppression of the Third World as he showed Remo the computer system that made this precinct twenty percent more effective than other New York City police precincts.

"We are an anticrime impact area. This is where the federal government has poured extra money into fighting crime."

"Like what?" asked Remo. He couldn't perceive any crime being fought.

"For one thing, with the extra money we sent sound trucks into the areas reconfirming the identity of Third World youth as oppressed victims of whites."

"You're white, aren't you?" asked Remo.

"Absolutely," said Pleskoff, "and ashamed of it." He seemed proud to be ashamed.

"Why? You had no more say in your becoming white than somebody else does in his becoming black," Remo said.

"Or any other similar lesser race," said Chiun, lest racist Americans confuse their lesser races with the better one which was yellow.

"I'm ashamed because of the great debt we owe to the great black race. Look," said Pleskoff confidentially. "I don't know the answers. I'm just a cop. I follow orders. There are people who are smarter than me. If I give the cockamamie answers, I get promoted. If, God forbid, I should ever let on that a black family moving onto your block isn't a blessing from Allah, I'd be cashiered. I live in Aspen, Colorado myself."

"Why Aspen? Why so far away?"

"Because I couldn't get to the pre-Civil War South," said Pleskoff. "Between you and me I used to root for the Rebels in those Civil War movies. Aren't you sorry we won now?"

"I want to know who killed the old woman, Mrs. Gerd Mueller of Walton Avenue," said Remo.

"I didn't know the FBI dealt in murder. What's federal about a killing?"

"It is a federal case. It's the most important case in the last two hundred years. It is very basic, as basic as the cave. The old and the weak are to be protected by their young men. Until recently, that's been the general mark of civilization. Maybe I've been paid to protect that old lady. Maybe the money she turned out of her pocketbook to pay my salary, your salary, maybe that just owes her that her killer doesn't waltz away to some psychiatric interview, if by some incredible accident he gets caught. Maybe, just maybe now with one little old white lady, the American people say 'enough.'"

"Gee, that's stirring," said Pleskoff. "To be honest, sometimes I want to help protect old people. But when you're a New York City cop, you can't do everything you want."

Pleskoff showed Remo the pride of the precinct, the main battle weapon in the new seventeen-million mass-impact, high-priority, anticrime battle. It was a $4.5 million computer.

"What does it do?"

"What does it do?" said Pleskoff proudly. "You say you want to know about a Mrs. Mueller, Gerd, homicide?" Pleskoff pressed a keyboard. He hummed. The machine spat out a stack of white cards into a metal tray. They fell there quietly, those twenty cards representing twenty deaths.

"Don't look so distraught, sir," said Pleskoff.

"Are those the elderly deaths for the city?" asked Remo.

"Oh, no," said Pleskoff. "Those are the Muellers. You ought to see the Schwartzes and the Sweeneys. You could play contract bridge with them."

Remo found cards for Mrs. Mueller and her husband.

"Homicide? Why is he in the homicide file?" Remo asked.

Pleskoff shrugged and looked at the card. "Okay, I see

now. Sometimes you'll have some old-timer who still believes in the old-fashioned direct limited link of victim-crime-killer. You know, the old way, criminal commit the crime, get the criminal? The mindless visceral irresponsible reaction that often leads to such atrocities as police riot."

"Which means?" asked Remo.

"Which means, this officer, this reactionary racist act an act of defiance against the department and his precinct mislabeled Gerd Mueller's death a murder. It was a heart attack."

"That's what I was told," said Remo. "I thought so."

"So did everyone except that racist. It was a heart attack, brought on by a knife injected into it. But you know how backward your traditional Irish cop is. Fortunately, they've got a union now and it helps enlighten them. You won't find them flying off the handle any more. Except if it's union business."

"Guess what?" said Remo. "You are about to identify a criminal. You are about to take me to the Saxon Lords. You are going to identify a killer."

"You can't make me do that. I'm a New York City policeman. We have union rules, you know."

Remo grabbed the lobe of Sergeant Pleskoff's right ear and twisted. It caused pain. Pleskoff smiled because the pain made him smile. Then he cried. Big tears came to his eyes.

"There's a very stiff penalty for assaulting a policeman," he gasped.

"When I find one in this remnant of a city, I promise I will not assault him."

Remo dragged the crying Sergeant Pleskoff from the stationhouse. The patrolmen behind the machine gun threatened to shoot because, in this case, it was legal.

"Don't think you're assaulting some ordinary citizen," yelled one patrolman. "That's a police officer and that

62

a crime. What do you think he is? Some rabbi or priest? That's a cop. There are laws against doing things to cops."

Remo noticed a large dark stain spread over the blue crotch of Sergeant Pleskoff. A New York City policeman had discovered to his horror that he was going to have to go out in the street after dark.

The night had cooled off. As soon as they were out of the stationhouse, the door bolted behind them.

"Oh God, what have I done? What have I done?" moaned Sergeant Pleskoff.

Chiun chuckled and said in Korean to Remo that he was fighting against a wave, instead of moving with it.

"I won't be the only one who drowns, Little Father," Remo said. And his voice was grim.

Chapter Five

Twisting an ear just before the tearing point is more secure than a rein. It is also a more effective information-gathering device. Keep the person who owned the ear just barely in pain—it did not have to be a lot of pain—and the person would start answering questions. On obvious lies, start the pain flowing again so that the person himself would make his body into a truth machine. It was not force that was required, but timing.

Sergeant Pleskoff, his right ear between Remo's fingers, thought the streets looked strange at night.

"This is a beat," said Remo. "You're going to walk it now."

Three black forms hovered in a doorway. A young girl called out at the door: "Ma, it's me. Let me in, you hear?"

One of the other dark forms was a young man. He held his hand to the girl's throat. In that hand, he held a cheap dime store saw with a pistol grip.

"That is a crime," whispered Remo, pointing across the darkened street.

"Yes. Bad housing is a crime against Third World peoples."

"No. No," said Remo. "You are not an economist. You are not a housing expert. You are a policeman. See. Someone is holding a saw to that girl's throat. That's your business."

"I wonder why he's doing that?"

"No. You're not a psychiatrist," said Remo and he began to twist Pleskoff's ear to the point of tearing. "Now think. What should you do?"

"Picket City Hall for jobs for young Afro-Americans?"

"No," said Remo.

"Demonstrate against racism?" said Sergeant Pleskoff, between gasps of pain.

"No racism there, Sergeant Pleskoff. That's black on black," said Remo. One of the men at the door with the young girl spotted Remo, Sergeant Pleskoff, and Chiun. Apparently he did not think the trio was worth bothering about. He turned back to the door waiting for the girl's mother to open it.

"Aw, right, Peaches," said the older man at the door. It was now time for threats. "We jam de lye up Delphinia's twat. Y'heah? Now you open dat mufu doah and spread yo' beaver 'cause it muvver and daughter night. Bofe of you be pleasured for de night."

"It's apparently a double rape with probable robbery coming up and I'd say a possible murder also," Remo said. "Wouldn't you, Chiun?"

"Wouldn't I what?" asked Chiun.

"Say it's those crimes."

"A crime is a matter of law," said Chiun. "I see two men overpowering a girl. Who knows what weapon she has? No. Crime requires that I judge right and wrong and the right I know is the way to breathe and move

65

and live. So are they right? No, they are all wrong for all of them breathe badly and move half asleep." Thus spake Oliver Wendell Chiun.

"See?" said Sergeant Pleskoff desperately.

"Arrest the men," said Remo.

"I'm one, they're two."

"You have a gun," said Remo.

"And endanger my retirement, my advancement points, my clothing allowance? They're not harming a policeman. That girl is too young to be a policeman."

"Either you use your gun on them or I use it on you," said Remo and released Sergeant Pleskoff's ear.

"Aha, you have threatened a police officer and are endangering a police officer," yelled Pleskoff and went for his gun. His hand shot down to the black handle and closed on it and ripped the .38 Police Special with the delicious heavy lead slug, creased down the middle to make a dumdum to splatter in his attacker's face. The bullet was not only illegal for New York City policemen, it had been made illegal for warfare by the Geneva Convention. But Sergeant Pleskoff knew he would only draw his gun in self-defense. You needed it when you left Aspen. He supported laws against handguns because he got advancement points for doing it. What difference did another law make? This was New York City. It had lots of laws, the most humanitarian laws in the country. But only one was in effect and Sergeant Pleskoff was going to enforce it now. The law of the jungle. He had been attacked, his ear had been brutalized, he had been threatened, and that FBI man who had gone bananas was going to pay for it.

But the gun seemed to float out of his hand and he was squeezing empty air. The FBI man, in the too-casual clothes for an FBI man, seemed to slide under and into the gun and then he had it. And he was offering it back, and Pleskoff took it back, and tried to kill him again and that didn't work either.

"Them or you," said Remo.

"Reasonable," said Sergeant Pleskoff, not quite sure whether this would be a proper defense before a police review board. It was just like a shooting range. Bang. The large one dropped, his head jerking like it was on a chain pulley. Bang. Bang. And he blew the spinal column out of the smaller one.

"I meant arrest them, you maniac," said Remo.

"I know," said Sergeant Pleskoff in a daze. "But I was afraid. I don't know why."

"It's okay, ma," yelled the girl and the door opened and a woman in a blue bathrobe peeked out.

"Thank the Lawd. You safe, chile?" she asked.

"De policemans, he do it," said the girl.

"God bless you, officer," yelled the woman, taking her daughter safely inside and bolting and reinforcing the locks.

A strange feeling overcame Sergeant Pleskoff. He couldn't describe it.

"Pride," said Remo. "Some cops have it."

"You know," said Pleskoff, excited. "We could get some of us down at the station house, on our off-hours, to walk the streets and do this sort of thing. In disguises, of course, so we wouldn't get reported to the commissioner. I know the old-timers used to do things like this, stop muggings and stuff, and shoot the shit out of anyone who endangers anyone else. Even if it isn't a cop. Let's get the Saxon Lords."

"I want to find out who did in Mrs. Mueller. So I've got to talk to them," Remo said. "Dead men don't talk."

"Fuck 'em. Shoot 'em all," said Pleskoff.

Remo took his gun away. "Just the bad guys."

"Right," said Pleskoff. "Can I reload?"

"No," said Remo.

"You know, I may not even get into trouble for this. Nobody has to know it was a policeman who stopped a robbery and rape. They could think it was a relative who shot up those two or maybe they didn't pay a Mafia loan shark. Then there would be no fuss at all."

This idea made Pleskoff happy. He was not sure whether the women would talk. But if word ever got back to the Reverend Josiah Wadson and the Black Ministry Council, then Pleskoff would lose his retirement pay. Perhaps even be fired.

If that happened, maybe he could go independent, offer a novel service of armed men protecting the unarmed. If this idea caught on, why, people without guns might be able to walk New York City's streets again. He did not know what this service might be called but one could always hire an advertising firm. Perhaps "Protecta-Block." Everyone on a block could chip in to pay for it. The men might even wear uniforms to distinguish themselves and let those who might harm people on the block know that there was protection there. It was a whiz-bang idea, thought Sergeant Pleskoff, and the good Lord knew New York City could use it.

Outside a schoolyard of concrete, surrounded by a high cyclone fence, Sergeant Pleskoff saw the dark blue denim jackets of the Saxon Lords. There were twenty or thirty of them moving along the fence. He did not have to read the lettering, even if he could on this dark night. Twenty or thirty dark jackets had to be the denim of the Saxon Lords. At first, he felt a fear of going on this street without their permission. Then he remembered he had a gun he could use. The man who had showed him the FBI Card held the gun for him. Pleskoff asked to reload.

"Those the Saxon Lords?" asked Remo.

"Yes. My gun," said Pleskoff.

"You use it before I tell you, you'll eat it," Remo said.

"Fair enough," said Pleskoff. His mind was feverish with possibilities for his unique Protecta-Block. The men protecting people could carry guns too. Like the one he had. There might even be a snappy name for these men in uniforms who carried guns and protected people, thought the New York City policeman, but he couldn't think of one right then. He filled the chambers of the gun with bullets.

Chiun watched the American policeman, then the group of young men. The young men walked with the confident arrogance of bullies. It was natural for man to herd but when he herded, what he gained in group strength he lost in individual courage.

"Who you?" demanded the tallest, revealing to Chiun and Remo that the gang was really disorganized. When the biggest ruled, it was a sign that physical prowess had to be used to gain leadership, not cunning or agreement. It was the same, then, as a gathering of strangers.

"Who am I, you mean," said Remo.

"Who you? Dat what I axed," said the tall one angrily.

"You want to know who I am. And I want to know who you are," said Remo.

"Dat mans need mannas," said the tall one.

"Manners, right?" said Remo. That's the word he thought it was.

"Let me take him," whispered Sergeant Pleskoff to Remo.

"De sergeant, he shoulda tol' you who de Saxon Lawds is, man. Ah sees de jive turkey, he wif you. We ain' got no street lights cause'a white oppression and 'trocities against de Tird Worl' Peoples. I gone be perfesser English when I learns to read. Head ob de department. Dey gotta has niggas. It's de law. Whole English 'partment, biggest in de worl'. De blacks invent de En-

69

glish, de whites done rob it from dems. You rip off, honkey."

"I'm not sure what you said but I understood that honkey part," Remo said, leveled two right fingers into the tall young man's navel and, finding the spinal column joint, severed it. There was hardly a whoosh from the collapsed lungs. The dark form doubled over, its shaggy head plopping into its pop brand-new sneakers with the Slam Dunk treads and the Super Soul super-sole of polyester and rubber. The sneakers had red stars on the insteps. If the tall young man had still had an operative nervous system, each eye could have seen at microscopic close distance, right under the instep star, the legend that the sneakers were made in Taiwan.

The nervous system also failed to pick up the loud metallic sound of a .45 caliber automatic clacking to the pavement that cool dark morning. The gun had come from the youth's right hand.

"Wha' happen? Wha', man?" The questions came from the young Saxon Lords as their leader stood only up to his waist, and then, in a slow moment, toppled forward in collapse, so that when he came to rest his legs were neatly pressed on top of him.

"He daid?" came a moaning voice. "De man's do a 'trocity on de brother."

"Shoot," said another. "I ain't seen nuffin'. Just another jive honkey with Sergean' Pleskoff. Hey, Pleskoff, wha' that in you hand?"

"No," said Remo to Sergeant Pleskoff. "Not yet."

There were two other guns of smaller caliber in the gang. Remo removed them, with stinging pain, from their holders. After the fourth gang member to fall in pain, the shouts about blood vengeance modified. On the fifth Afro snapping back like a wild dust mop on a tight spring, the tenor of the game changed from threats to obeisance, from master to slave, from macho postur-

70

ing to "no sirs" and head scratching, and they were just standing here innocent at four A.M., minding their own business. Waitin' to see if some nice white man should come along so they could help. Yessuh.

"Empty your pockets and put your hands up on that fence," said Sergeant Pleskoff. He grinned with delirious pleasure. "I wish I had twenty pair of those things. The kind of things that go on wrists and lock. The whatchamacallits."

"Handcuffs," said Remo.

"Yeah, right. Handcuffs," Pleskoff said.

Remo asked about the house that had been torn down. Nobody knew anything about the building. Remo broke a finger. And very quickly he found out that the building had been in Saxon Lord territories, the gang had hit the Muellers a few times, the man had been knifed, but no one here had done the final one on Mrs. Mueller. Lordy, no. No one here would do anything like that.

"Was it another gang?" asked Remo.

"No," came the answer. Remo broke another finger.

"All right," he said. "Who did Mueller? Who did the old man?"

There were murmurings over exactly which old white man Remo meant.

"De one dat cried, begged, and cried not to slam him no more? Dat white man? Or de one whats bleed de carpets like puddles?"

"The one with the German accent," Remo said.

"Raht. De one dat talks funny," said one.

As near as Remo could determine, there had been two old white men in that building. The Saxon Lords killed the first because he wouldn't tell them where his insulin needle was hidden. The second, seeing that they were about to successfully enter his apartment, threw himself at them.

71

A young man grinned at how that seventy-year-old man tried to fight.

"You were there?" Remo said.

"Ah was. He were funny, dat old man."

"Try a younger one," Remo said and wiped the grin out onto the sidewalk in little white pellets of teeth and with his right hand cupped like the top of a juicer, pushed the face into the schoolyard fence like potatoes through a masher. The head stuck. The body dangled. The fence quivered and it was established at this point on 180th Street off Walton Avenue in the Bronx that frail old white people struggling for life were not humorous matters.

"All right, now we'll try again. Who killed Mrs. Mueller?"

"Idi Amin," said one young man.

"I thought I warned you about joking," Remo said.

"I not joking. Idi Amin, he our leader, he de one you kills ober dere." He pointed to where the gang's leader lay on the schoolyard pavement like a closed-up jacknife.

"He did it? Mrs. Mueller?" asked Remo.

"Dat right, boss. He do it."

"Alone? Don't tell me alone. None of you could find your way down a flight of stairs alone."

"Not alone, mistuh. Big-Big. He do it too."

"Who's Big-Big?" Remo asked.

"Big-Big Pickens. He do it."

"Which one of you is Big-Big Pickens?"

"He not here, suh. He away."

"Away where?"

"He go to Newark. When all de mens comes and starts looking around de old people's building, Big-Big, he decide go Newark till it safe to come back."

"Where in Newark?" Remo said.

"Nobody know. Nobody find no one single nigger in Newark."

Remo nodded to that. He would wait for Big-Big. Sergeant Pleskoff shined a small penlight on the cement sidewalk. It looked as if someone had thrown a drugstore at the feet of the teenagers leaning against the schoolyard fence. Pill bottles, envelopes with white powder, doodads, and a small shriveled gray lump.

"What's that?" asked Pleskoff.

"A human ear," said Chiun, who had seen what they looked like in China where bandit kidnapers sent first a finger asking for ransom, and if the ransom was not paid, sent an ear signifying the captive's death.

"Whose?" asked Remo.

"Mine," said a boy who could not be over fourteen years old.

"Yours?" asked Remo.

"Yeah. I got it. Offen de subway. It mine." Remo looked at one side of the boy's head, then the other. Both his ears were there.

"Ah cuts de ears. Dey mine."

"Enough," yelled Remo, rage surging through him, and he struck dead center into the black face. But Sinanju was not a way of rage, but of perfection.

The hand went with the speed of a nerve transmission but the precision and the rhythm was jarred by the hate. The hand crushed the skull and dug into the warm wet unused brain, but in piercing the bone at such speed without the usual rhythm, a bone snapped and the return of the hand slowed and it came back with blood and pain.

"Enough," said Chiun. "You have misused Sinanju and now look. Look at the hand I trained. Look at the body I trained. Look at the angry furious wounded animal you have become. Like any other white man."

Hearing that, one of the young blacks yelled, out of reflex: "Right on."

Chiun, the Master of Sinanju, silenced this rude interruption of a private conversation. It looked as if the long delicate fingernails floated ever so slowly at the wide nose but when the yellow hand touched the black face, it was as if the head had met a baseball bat at full swing. He dropped and spattered like a fresh egg being cracked into a hot frying pan.

And Chiun spoke to Remo. "Take one of these boys and I will show you how futile and childish is your justice. Justice is beyond any man and but an illusion. Justice? Have you done justice by wasting awesome talents on these things, obviously of no use to anyone else and even less use to themselves? What justice? Come."

"The hand doesn't hurt," said Remo. He held his shoulder so that not even the resonance of his breathing should reach past his wrist into that most delicate area of explosive pain. He knew his lie was useless because he himself had been taught where a man pained. It was visible in the body trying to protect it and his shoulder was hunched over his right hand so that it hung vertical and still. Oh, still, please, still, thought Remo, who had believed he had forgotten pain like this.

"Pick one," said Chiun, and Remo pointed to a form in the darkness.

So it was here that they left with Tyrone Walker, sixteen, also known as Alik Al Shaboor, the Hammer, Sweet Tye, and three other names, none of which, Remo would find out later, Tyrone could spell the same way twice. Chiun and Remo also parted with Sergeant Pleskoff who, carried away with his zeal for ending violence on the streets, at 3:55 A.M. stopped a very tough-looking black man with a bullet head and shoulders like walls. He was accompanied in a gold Cadillac by four

74

other blacks. The man made a sudden movement, and Sergeant Pleskoff unloaded his .38 Special into the head of a Teaneck orthodontist and the rest of the car: two accountants, a rustproofing representative, and the deputy superintendent of the Weequahic Waterways Commission.

When Pleskoff heard about it on television the next day, he worried about being discovered. Ballistics might be checked, just like in Chicago. For shooting five innocent men in a car, a New York City police officer could be suspended for weeks. But these were black men. Pleskoff might lose his job entirely.

Tyrone left with the two white men. The yellow man was light enough to be white anyhow. Tyrone didn't know. He threatened to do harm to the two, so the white one with the hurt hand slapped him with the other.

Tyrone stopped threatening. They took him to a hotel room. Oh, that was the action these two queers wanted. Tyrone was not about to be raped.

"Fifty dollar," said Tyrone. Otherwise it would be male rape.

"The old man wants you and he doesn't want you for that," said the younger white man who had done the 'trocity on the Saxon Lords.

They asked Tyrone if he were hungry. He sure was. This big hotel was right off the park in Downtown. It was called the Plaza. It had big old fancy rooms. It had a real nice-looking eating room downstairs. Like a Colonel Sanders except people brought the food. It real good.

Alik Al Shaboor, né Tyrone Walker, ordered a Pepsi and a Twinkie.

The white man ordered Tyrone a steak and vegetables. He ordered plain rice for himself. Why the white man order them things that Tyrone, he doan want?

"Because sugar does you no good," said the white man.

Tyrone, he watch de yellow man run dem long funny fingers over the hurt finger ob de white man. It sure look funny but de white man, he just settle down and de finger, it hurt him no moah. Lahk magic.

The food came. Tyrone ate the bread and the crackers. The white man, he tell Tyrone to eat everyfin on de plate. Tyrone let de white man know what he can do wif de plate. De white man, he grab Tyrone's ear. It hurt, real bad it hurt. Ooooweee. It hurt.

Tyrone real hungry. Tyrone eat it all. But all. Including the white stringy, thing, that hard to cut.

In a stroke of reason, it dawned on Tyrone that if he rolled the white stringy thing into balls after cutting it into strips, he could swallow the white thing more easily.

"Don't eat the napkin, stupid," Remo said.

"Ah," said Chiun. "He does not know your Western ways. And that is part of my proof that you cannot do justice. Even if he had killed the old woman whom you did not know, but have taken such cause for, his death could not bring her back to her life."

"I can make sure the killer doesn't enjoy his."

"But is that justice?" asked Chiun. "I cannot do justice, but you Remo, many years away from even fifty years, you will do justice." He nodded to the youth. "I give you this as typical. Its name is Tyrone. Could you give this justice?"

Tyrone spat out the last strand of napkin. He sure wished the white man had told him not to eat it right off.

"You," said Chiun. "Talk about yourself, for we must know who you are."

Since the two men could hurt him physically and they

weren't teachers or cops who didn't mean anything to anyone, Tyrone answered.

"Ah wants to go find my great ancestor kings, kings of Africa, Muslim kings."

"You want to trace it back like *Heritage?*" asked Remo, referring to a popular book of invention, how a black supposedly had found the village of his ancestors. If a novel had had that many factual errors, it would have been questioned, even for fiction. This one sold as nonfiction, even though it had cotton being grown in America before it was a crop, it had slaves being brought directly to America instead of being shipped to the islands first as was the real manner, and most laughably, it had a black slave being shipped back to England for training, during a time when any such slave would have been freed under English law. It was now a textbook in colleges. Remo had read the book and admired the writer's persistence. He himself did not know his heritage, who had been left at an orphanage at birth.

This was one of the reasons that CURE had selected him as its enforcement arm. No one would miss him. And in truth, he had no one but Chiun. And yet in Chiun, he had everyone, his own heritage which now joined with Sinanju, stretched back over thousands of years. Remo didn't care whether *Heritage* was true or not. He wanted it to be true. What harm could it do anyone if the book were really nonsense? Maybe people needed it.

"Ah knows ah can find the great Muslim king whats my heritage if ah gets the most difficult part of it. Ah can do it. Ah sho can do it."

"What's the difficult part?" asked Remo.

"All de Saxon Lawds, we got that first hard part in going back a hundred years. A thousand years."

"What hard part?" Remo asked again.

"We can get back to the great Muslim kings of Africa, oncet we gets our fathers. Piggy, he got it closest of all. He know his father got to be one outta three men. He real close."

Chiun raised a finger. "You will use your mind, creature. And you will see before you an old white woman. There are two pictures you will see. One, she closes the door and walks away. The other, she lies dead at your feet. Still and dead. Now, which is a bad picture?"

"Closin' de door, dat be bad."

"Why?" said Chiun.

"Cause she gots her money. Other way, she be daid and ah gots her money."

"Is it not wrong to kill old people?" Chiun asked. He smiled.

"No. Dey de best. You gets de young men, and dey can kill you. Ole people, dey de best. No trouble, specially iffen dey white."

"Thank you," said Chiun. "And you, Remo, would kill this one and call it justice?"

"You're damned right," said Remo.

"This is not a person talking," said Chiun pointing to the young black man in the blue denim jacket with Saxon Lords on the back. "Justice is for persons. But this is not a person. Not even a bad person. A bad person would do what this one has done, but even a bad person would know it was wrong to do it. This thing has no idea that it is wrong to hurt the weak. You cannot do justice to something less than human. Justice is a human concept."

"I don't know," Remo said.

"He right," said Tyrone, sensing impending release. He had been through family court thirteen times and he knew freedom when he saw it.

78

"Would you kill a giraffe for eating a leaf?" asked Chiun.

"If I were a farmer, I'd sure as hell keep giraffes away from my trees. I'd probably shoot them," Remo said.

"Perhaps. But do not call it justice. Not justice. You cannot punish a leaf for reaching to the light and you cannot do justice to a pear that ripens and falls off a tree. Justice is done to men who have choices."

"I don't think this thing here should live," said Remo.

"And why not?" Chiun asked.

"Because he's a disaster waiting to happen."

"Perhaps," said Chiun, smiling. "But as I said, you are an assassin, the strong deadly arm of emperors. You are not the man who keeps the sewers flowing. That is not your job."

"No suh. You ain' de sewer man. De sewer man. De sewer man. No suh, you ain' de sewer man." Tyrone popped his fingers to his little jingle. His body bounced on the expensive gold and white chair.

Remo looked at the young man. There were many like him. What difference would one more make?

His right hand was numbed but he knew it had been set with more skill than any bone surgeon, and he knew it was healing with the speed of a baby's bone. When your body lived to its maximum, it used itself more efficiently. The hand would heal but would he anger again during work? He looked at his hand and at Tyrone.

"Do you understand what we're talking about?" Remo asked Tyrone.

"Ah doan unnerstan' all dat jive talk."

"Well, jive on this, pal. I think I ought to kill you in return for the crimes you've committed against the world, the worst of which was being born. I think that's justice. Now Chiun here thinks you should live because you're an animal, not a human, and justice has nothing to do with animals. What do you think?"

"Ah thinks ah better get outta heah."

"Hold that thought, Tyrone," Remo said. "You're going to stay alive for awhile, while I decide whether I'm right or Chiun's right."

"Take yo' time. No sense hurrying."

Remo nodded. "Now, some questions. If something was stolen from an apartment during a killing, where would it wind up?"

Tyrone hesitated.

"You're getting ready to lie, Tyrone," said Remo. "That's what people do, not animals. Lie and you're people. Be people, and you're dead, because I'll do justice on you. Understand?"

"Anything what gets stole, it goes to de Revin Wadson."

"What's D. Revin Wadson?" Remo asked.

"Not D. Revin," Tyrone said. "De revin."

"He means the reverend," Chiun said. "I have learned a great deal about this dialect in the last hour."

"Who is he?" asked Remo.

"He a preacher, a big mucky-muck wit housing and like dat."

"And he's a fence?"

"Evybody gots make a libbin'."

"Chiun, who should be responsible for him?" Remo asked. "Who's supposed to teach him that thieving and killing and rape and robbery are wrong?"

"Your society should. All civilized societies do that. They set standards that people should live up to."

"Like schools, parents, churches?" Remo asked.

Chiun nodded.

"You go to school, Tyrone?" Remo asked.

" 'Course ah goes to school."

"To read and things like that?"

"Ah doan read. Ah ain' gone be no brain surgeon. De

80

brain surgeons, dey read. You watch dey lips in de subways. Dey readin' de get-outta-dem signs."

"You know anybody who reads without moving his lips?" Remo asked.

"Not at Malcolm-King-Lumumba High School. You wants some smartass honkey, dey reads up at Bronx High."

"There are other people in the world who read without moving their lips. In fact, most readers don't."

"De Tom blacks. Uncle Tom, Aun' Jemima, dey apin' de whites. Ah can count to a thousand, wanna hear me?"

"No," said Remo.

"One hundred, two hundred, three hundred, four . . ."

Remo thought about welding Tyrone's two lips together. Tyrone stopped counting to a thousand by hundreds. He saw the glint in Remo's eyes and he wasn't looking for pain.

When the phone rang in their suite upstairs, Remo answered. Chiun watched Tyrone for here was something new. A creature that looked human in form but had no humanity in its soul. He would have to study this one and pass on his wisdom to the next Masters of Sinanju so those Masters would have one less thing new to encounter. It was the new things that could destroy you. There was no greater advantage than familiarity.

"Smitty," said Remo. "I'm close to finding your gadget, I think."

"Good," came the acid voice. "But there's something bigger out there. One of our foreign operating agencies picked up something in Moscow communications. At first we thought Russia was ignorant of all this, and then we found out they were a bit too cute. They sent a man. A Colonel Speskaya."

"I don't know every spitting Russian ding dong," said Remo.

"Well, he's a colonel at age twenty-four and they just don't make people colonels at that age. If that's any help."

"I got enough with my job without keeping up with Russian administration," Remo said.

Chiun nodded sagely. The most American thing about Americans was that they tried to change everything, especially when it worked well enough already. Thus, seeing the beautiful handiwork of the Master of Sinanju in transforming Remo, they constantly tried to make Remo, the assassin, into something else. Not that the other things were unworthy. But anyone with enough effort could become a detective or a spy. It took special qualities to be an assassin. It was good to see Remo resisting the obscene blandishments of Smith. Chiun nodded at Remo, letting him know he was doing the right thing in resisting Smith's nonsense.

"They sent the colonel," Smith said, "and they did it beautifully. We thought they weren't interested in the Mueller device at all, but they were. But now, our intercepts tell us they found something better. Two instruments that are better and more important than the Mueller thing."

"So now I'm not just looking for the device that the Mueller family had, but I'm looking for a Colonel Speskaya and two new weapons he's got his hands on?"

"Yes. Precisely," said Smith.

"Smitty. This job isn't worth spit." Remo happily hung up the phone. When it rang again, he tore it out of the socket. When a bellboy came up to check the phone out of order, Remo gave him fifty dollars and told him to leave the suite of rooms alone. When the assistant manager came up and insisted a phone be reinstalled, Remo allowed as how life was hard and he wanted to get some sleep and if he were bothered again, he would install the phone in the assistant manager's face.

The suite was not bothered again that night. Remo locked Tyrone Walker in the bathroom. With some newspapers on the floor.

Chapter Six

The Reverend Josiah Wadson let his booming voice resonate out over the auditorium in the Bronx. Outside long lines of moving vans were parked, their engines stilled, their carriers locked. They had distant license plates, from Delaware, Ohio, Minnesota, Wyoming, but each had fresh canvas signs: "Affirmative Housing II, Rev. J. Wadson, Executive Director."

Inside the auditorium, elderly white people sat listening to the reverend. Box lunches of fried chicken and rich dripping ribs, with crusty white bread, had been passed out and they drank milk and coffee and soft drinks.

"I prefer tea and toast," said one woman with a twang that crackled with age. She wore a delicate sapphire ring with small diamond baguettes set in white gold, the sort of tiny delicacy of a world even older than hers. She smiled and said please, because all her life she had always said please. She could not remember not saying it.

Nor would she ever fail to say thank you. It was a just and proper thing. People should treat each other with respect, which was why she was here today from Troy, Ohio.

There were good and bad in all races and if whites were needed so that all men could be equal, then, like her great-grandfather who fought to end slavery, so would she volunteer herself. And the government was being very generous. They would pay half her rent for a year. It was called Affirmative Housing II, and Rebecca Buell Hotchkiss of Troy, Ohio looked forward to what she had told her friends was a new challenge.

She was going to meet a whole new world of friends of different-colored skin. If they were half as nice as Mr. and Mrs. Jackson, her close black friends in Troy, why then she had just stumbled into a windfall. When she thought of New York City she thought of all the shows she could see. All the museums she could visit.

Why, they had television in New York City on almost all the channels. And the Botanical Gardens and the Bronx Zoo were within just a few miles of where she would be living. Her furniture was outside in one of the vans and here were other nice people from all over America, going to show that America believed in brotherhood. What could go wrong? Josiah Wadson was a reverend and he was directing this lovely people program.

So she asked, with a very big please, for tea and toast. She did not like ribs and chicken. It was too harsh for her queasy stomach.

She asked this of one of the nice young men. She thought all the people she had met were nice. And she refused to believe there was anything evil about the reverend wearing a pistol. After all, there were many racists around and as a little girl she knew how hard it could be on Negro men at that time. Whooops. Black. She

85

would have to learn that was the nice thing to call them now. Whooops. You did not refer to blacks as "them." She was learning.

She was surprised when she was refused tea and toast.

"You don' like ribs and chicken 'cause you a racist," said the young man. He looked at her hand the way other young men used to look at her bosom. It was the hand with the ring her grandmother had given her.

"I used to love southern food," said Miss Hotchkiss, "but now I have a queasy stomach."

This small commotion was heard on the stage of the auditorium by Reverend Wadson. He had his pistol buttoned under his black jacket. He wanted to know what the trouble was down there. The young man told him.

"Well, let her have tea and toast. If she wants to deny the rich black heritage being offered her for her pale white tea and toast, let her. We on to an enrichment program for whites."

Wadson grinned a big licorice happiness as the auditorium returned him polite applause.

"De white man, he need to complicate thing. It 'bout time, we moralize him. We fight complication wif clarity. Evil wif morality. We give de white oppressor a moral standard he never know."

The whites applauded with alacrity but not with enthusiasm. The applause came and went like a dutiful blast from a pistol shot. Loud and short.

"Affirmative Housing Two, it simple. No need to muggy up wif high-falutiness. It simple as grits. Housin', it segregated. Segregation, it against de law. All of you be criminals. Till now. Now, you be paid to follow de law of de land. Law, it say you gotta live wif nigg ... with blacks," and on this note, Reverend Wadson bellowed into glorious resonance.

"How looong, Oh Lawd, de black man gotta do de integrating? How long, oh Lawd, de black man he gotta go integrating? No longer, Lawd. Lawd, ah gots good news for you now. At long last, ah gots good news for yo' bleedin' heart. Black consciousness and black pride bring de oppressor 'round to do what legal and right. Whites, dey gonna do de integrating."

And with a cautionary note to the ruler of the universe that the whites had to be offered moving money to move into black neighborhoods, the Reverend Wadson concluded by asking a blessing on getting whites to do what they should have done from the beginning.

Affirmative Housing II was quite simply integration of neighborhoods using whites instead of blacks as the integrators, and black neighborhoods instead of white ones as the areas to be integrated. It was an experimental pilot project of Rev. Wadson's Black Ministry Council, funded by the federal government. There was six million dollars for the project. Urban economists call the grant "so little they don't want it to work."

Of the six million dollars, two million went for consulting fees, one million for the moving, two million for exploratory research and nine hundred thousand dollars for "outreach, input, and counterface groupings." The remaining one hundred thousand dollars went to buy two buildings, the owner of which gave Reverend Wadson an envelope with forty thousand dollars in it as a sales commission, sometimes referred to, when indulged in by whites, as a kickback.

The strategy sessions called workshops were conducted at resorts in Trinidad, Puerto Rico, Jamaica, Cannes, and Paris. There were floods of consultants and consulting firms at one hundred dollars per hour. Many of the finest New York City courtesans found themselves giving advice on interrace counterfaces.

This auditorium was costing American taxpayers forty

thousand dollars in consulting fees. Besides Reverend Wadson, there were black authorities and consultants sensitizing the white audience. There was talk on *Heritage*, which showed blacks were good and whites were bad and how ignoble whites had ruined noble black men. The black speaker had written a review of this book and for five thousand dollars he read his review.

It said he didn't know why the author bothered to give unworthy whites such a worthy book. He blamed whites for not bringing up blacks as Muslims. He said he didn't know why he even bothered to talk to the whites, because nobody else cared for whites. Not in the whole world.

The author carried a pocketbook and looked like a popeyed toad. He smoked with a vengeance. Reverend Wadson thanked him and made the audience thank him.

The program was named Affirmative Housing II because there had been an Affirmative Housing I. The two million dollars for consulting fees in this program had shown that Affirmative Housing I had failed because the whites were inadequately sensitized to black culture. Now they were being sensitized.

They all watched a film on how bad whites were to blacks in the South before civil rights.

They watched a dance troupe perform "Revolutionary Black Vanguard." It showed black revolutionaries killing white oppressors like priests and nuns.

Miss Hotchkiss saw all this and told herself that perhaps she had negative feelings because she wasn't sensitive enough.

A poet read about burning white venom wombs with black righteousness. Burning houses down around whites. Revolution. No more Jesus. Gimme Marx.

A comedian now calling himself a "conscience activist" explained how the FBI had acted peculiarly during the assassination of Martin Luther King. The FBI, said the comedian, had leaked out a story that the good reverend didn't stay in black hotels. And out of the goodness of the reverend's heart, when he heard this story, he moved to a black hotel where he was assassinated. Therefore the FBI was to blame. The comedian was paid three thousand dollars for this lecture.

There was a picture of Field Marshal Doctor Idi Amin Dada, President for Life, on stage and a recording of his voice telling the audience that he really liked whites and that they shouldn't be fooled by propaganda from whites.

Then there was the interview for Afro News television, called "Like It Really Is," and there was Reverend Wadson's serious face and sonorous voice.

"We trying, Lawd, we trying, to counteract in this brief afternoon years of racist propaganda." The female announcer said to the camera whirring away that everyone agreed it was an uphill fight to counteract racist propaganda. She said that if Reverend Wadson were successful in his struggle, then there would be no need for busing because then America would be integrated. "We all know the reverend for his good fight against police barbarousness and atrocities," she said.

Then the whites were ushered out of the auditorium and told to smile at the cameras. But since Swedish television was late arriving, the elderly whites were herded again back into the auditorium. Then they were guided out again, but since there weren't enough smiles, they were pushed back in and told to come out again, smiling. A few fainted. Miss Hotchkiss kept going by holding on to the man in front of her.

Someone yelled for them to smile. She tried to. Young black men in black leather jackets stood in rows. The tired old people were marched up to the rows of men and got threats that those who did not smile would suffer.

Miss Hotchkiss heard words she had never heard before. She tried smiling. If one were pleasant, if others knew you meant only pleasantness, then certainly basic human dignity would prevail. An old man from Des Moines began sobbing.

"It will be all right," said Miss Hotchkiss. "It will be all right. Remember, all men are brothers. Didn't you hear how moral blacks are? What do we have to fear from people who are morally superior? Don't worry," she said but she did not like the way the young black men eyed her sapphire ring. She would have taken it off if she could. But it had not been able to slip off since she was seventeen. She told herself it was such a small ring, scarcely a few points of a carat. It had come over from England with an ancestor, who had brought it west through the Erie Canal and down into the Miami, Ohio valley, where good people had made good land bountiful.

Her great-grandfather had gone to war and lost a leg to free blacks from slavery. And the ring was his mother's, given to Miss Hotchkiss over the passage of time. It was important, because it tied her to her past. Yet now the woman, rich in years but poor in the youthful sap that made climbing into a bus a simple procedure, would very much have wanted to have left that ring with her sister's child. She felt the ring endangered her life.

She was relieved to see a man with a collar get on the bus. He had a round jovial face. He said he wanted everyone to hear his version of the Good Samaritan.

"A man was walking along the road when another man jumped on him and robbed him of everything and then demanded to know why he was poor," said the man with the collar. Miss Hotchkiss was confused. She remembered the Good Samaritan as helping someone. She didn't understand.

"I see you're confused. You are the robbers. And the Third World has been robbed by you. Whites have made the Third World oppressed, poor by robbing them."

A man with silver hair raised a hand. He was an economics teacher, he said. He had been teaching thirty years and was retired. He said that while there were faults with colonization, it was a fact that it did raise the life expectancy of the native population.

"Poverty and starvation in the Third World is really just slightly better than it's always been. They are living the life of preindustrialized man. Nobody stole anything from them. They never had it. Wealth is an invention of the industrial society."

"What about natural resources?" yelled the man with the collar. "That's stealing on a massive scale. Robbing the inalienable right to a resource."

"Actually, no," said the white-haired economics teacher, patiently, as if explaining dry underwear to a bedwetter. "What you're talking about are colored stones and things in the ground that preindustrialized man has no use for anyhow. Industrialized man not only pays him for it, but pays him to use his labor in mining it or drilling for it. The problem is that preindustrialized man has been exposed to the richer life of industrialized man and naturally he wants it. But he's got to work at it. The fact is nobody stole anything from anybody."

"Racist," screamed the man in the collar. "You're not allowed to believe things like that. Out of the program."

"Fine. I just don't want this anyway. I found out I don't like you people. I don't trust you people and I don't want anything to do with you people," said the white-haired man, his voice quivering.

91

"Get out," screamed the man with the collar and since the television cameras had gone and would not record the moment, the man was allowed to get off the bus, with veiled hints about his never being able to recover his furniture again. Miss Hotchkiss wanted to go with him. But there was the cherrywood cabinet that Aunt Mary had given her and that table that had come up with the family along the Erie Canal. It would be all right. She knew so many nice Negro people in Troy, Ohio.

Had she given up the family furniture, Miss Hotchkiss might have spared herself a death of horror. She was going to lose the furniture anyway. The world was going to lose that furniture. The economics teacher, with a wisdom people often get in the valley of death, realized that there was a chance to get new furniture only if he were alive.

In a program where it was mandatory to blame all whites for everything and forbidden to blame any black for anything, he knew the whites were becoming the new Jews for the new black Nazis.

He willingly gave up his entire wallet and emptied his pockets at the door of the bus to a young black man. Did the young man want his buttons? He could have them too.

Later, the New York City police would blame the disaster of Affirmative Housing II on the late start of the buses toward the multiracial living environments, which meant the two slum buildings the program owned.

The buses and the vans got there at dark. The drivers of the vans, later to be blamed by the mayor for cowardice, fled in a group as night descended. The bus drivers hailed gypsy cabs.

And the white settlers were left in the buses parked in front of the vans. A young black boy found he could jimmy open the side of one of the buses. Gangs of black youths swarmed aboard and dragged the elderly whites out of the buses. Some had to regrab because old people's hair came out so easily. Miss Hotchkiss clung to one of the metal legs of the seats welded to the floor.

But she could not hold when the boot stamped down on her wrist, crushing old and fragile bone. The pain was young and new and she shrieked, but hardly anyone heard her screams for mercy because everyone was screaming.

She felt her right hand with the ring being lifted up and felt herself thrown around as several young black men fought for her.

Someone had gotten into the vans and was throwing the furniture onto a giant bonfire of flame that roared almost as high as the tenements around her. She felt a sharp tearing at her ring finger and knew the finger was no longer there. She felt herself being lifted up and the flames enveloped her, very yellow and burning hot, so that there was a sudden blasting pain, and then, surprisingly, nothing.

One black woman in a third-story apartment dialed 911, Police Emergency.

"Get down here. Get down here. They're burning people. They're burning people at Walton and 173rd."

"How many people are being burned?" asked the policeman.

"I don' know. A dozen. Two dozen. Oh, God. It terrible."

"Lady, we'll get down as soon as we can. We're understaffed. We've got bigger disasters ahead of you."

"Dey burning' whites. Now will you get somebody down heah? Dey got de Saxon Lawds, de Stone Shieks of Allah, all de gangs. It horrible. Dey burning people."

"Thank you for reporting," came the voice and the

phone clicked off. The black women drew the curtains and cried. There were times as a child in Orangeburg, South Carolina, when she couldn't go out in the street safely because she was black. And that was bad. There was no great joy in coming north, but there had been hope.

Now, just when the greatest hopes were being achieved, she couldn't walk out in the streets except in the early morning. And she did not relish the screams of whites any more than of blacks.

She just thought that people ought to be left alone with a bit of dignity, and if not dignity, at least a little safety. But she didn't even have that. She opened an old family bible and she read and she prayed for everyone. Someone had said there was a lot of money spent fighting poverty. Well, she was poor and she didn't see any of it. Someone said there was a lot of money spent fighting racism. Well, if she were white and she were bused into some of the trash that made her life miserable, she certainly wasn't going to hate blacks less.

Now, if someone wanted to fight racism, they ought to have decent whites meet decent, God-fearing black people. There was nothing like decent people meeting decent people. When the screams penetrated her room, she went into the bathroom. And when she could still hear the screams of people being burned alive, she shut the bathroom door and let the water run. And there she prayed.

Reverend Wadson prayed too. He prayed for a softening of white hearts. He did this from a podium in a ballroom of the Waldorf-Astoria Hotel, rented by Affirmative Housing II, as an antiracism workshop. To help fight racism, there was a ten-piece band, three rock singers, and an open bar.

Television cameras focused on Reverend Wadson's massive perspiring rutty face over the white collar. The eyes rolled and the lips glistened under the ballroom lights. His nostrils flared wide enough and round enough to hide a pair of giant immies in his nose. Reverend Wadson was like a freight train, at first punching out single thoughts at a slow steady pace and then rising in pitch and speed. And what he said was that America was abandoning its fight against oppression. But there was a way the fight could be continued. How? Quite logically. By funding Affirmative Housing III, with meaningful amounts of money.

"When de man, he lay down six million to solve three hundred year of oppression, he sayin' ah doan wan' innegration to succeed. No, suh. He sayin' in his six million ways, niggah, you go starve. But de Third World, it know de man. It know he immoral. It know de rich black contribution to de world ain' gonna be ripped off by de white man."

"So you're saying that the federal government's program is so badly funded as to border on fraud," said the Swedish television announcer, her hair as cool yellow as pale wheat stalks, her skin the white smooth cream of the North people, her teeth even and unravaged by cavity or brace. A shimmering black silk pants suit highlighted full and ready breasts and driving derriere. Even while she stood still, the black silk moved up and down her leg. Her perfume enveloped Reverend Wadson.

"Dat exactly what I been sayin'," Wadson said.

"You have been so helpful, Reverend, to Swedish television," the blond said. "I wish we could have more of your time."

"Who say you can't?" asked the reverend. He was a big man, at least six-feet-four and he seemed to throw his whole body into her face.

"Don't you have a lecture tonight on the beauty of black women?" she asked. Reverend Wadson took twenty seconds to mouth the letters on the name tag pinned to the beautiful rising black silk covering what must be a mountain of white breast.

"Ingrid," he said, looking up to make sure by watching her face that he had said it correctly. "Ingrid, I think sisterhood powerful. Powerful. Powerful. I with you in sisterhood."

A black woman in stylish but hard-lined dashiki with elegant barren copper jewelry around her long ebony neck and with short hair in black rows, tugged at the sleeve of Reverend Wadson.

"Reverend, your lecture. Remember, you're a consultant to the city on race relations."

"I busy," said Wadson and smiled at the blond.

"But you are part of the program. You are a consultant to the city," said the black woman.

"Later," said Reverend Wadson.

"But your lecture is about the city's fight against racism," said the woman. She smiled politely but firmly at the Swedish television announcer.

"Later, I said. We workin' international now," said Reverend Wadson who placed a large hand on the silk-covered shoulder of Ingrid. Ingrid smiled. Reverend Wadson saw her breasts peak under the black silk. She wasn't wearing a bra.

"Reverend," said the black woman, her lips pursing. "There are many people who want to hear you talk on beauty and black being synonymous."

"Synonymous? Ah never calls it synonymous. Never. Black beauty your basic beauty. It ain' synonymous. Too long, oh Lawd, has our beautiful black beauties been called synonymous by white racists. Ingrid, we gots get outta here and talk about racism and beauty."

"Synonymous means 'the same as,'" said the black woman. "Black is the same as beauty, beauty is black. Black is beauty."

"Right on," said Reverend Wadson, turning his back on the woman and guiding Ingrid into his path.

"Reverend, New York City pays you forty-nine thousand dollars a year for your lectures," said the woman tugging the back of Wadson's dark ministerial coat.

"I busy, woman," said Reverend Wadson.

"Reverend, I'm not letting you go," said the woman.

"I be back, Ingrid. Doan you go nowhere, heah?"

"I will be here," said the Swedish beauty and gave Wadson a big wink. The reverend went into an administrative room of the hotel to talk to the black woman who was helping him in his lecture series to colleges in the city.

"This only take a minute," said Reverend Wadson who had played tight end for a black college in the south and was known to be able to unfoot someone with one swipe. He slammed the black woman's head against the wall. She dropped like a sack of soggy week-old collards.

Wadson returned to Ingrid. A group of young blacks had gathered around her. With bulk strength, Reverend Wadson cleared them away. And still chuckling, he brought Ingrid to a conference room where he finally got his hands on the black silk and undraped it away from the soft white body that he covered with his anxious tongue. And just before his triumph, she wriggled away and he lunged for her. But she was too fast. She claimed he really didn't want her.

Want her? Was that a droop of disinterest, Wadson wanted to know?

She consented but only after he promised his help.

"Sho. Anyfing," panted the Reverend Wadson. "First dis."

Ingrid smiled her perfect smooth-skinned smile. Reverend Wadson thought at that moment she needed no skin lighteners. Never a lotion on that face.

She asked to kiss him.

He allowed as that would be all right.

Down went the zipper of his trousers. Ingrid reached up and brought her long hair behind her head in two handfuls.

Reverend Wadson lunged forward, body and desire out of control.

Suddenly Ingrid pulled back.

"Drop your gun, Reverend," she said and gone was the lilt of Sweden from her voice.

"Hah?" Wadson said.

"Drop that gun you're carrying," she repeated. "A gorilla with a gun is dangerous."

"Bitch," said the reverend and was about to bang her yellow head into the furniture when he felt a tingle around a very delicate part of his body. It was as if she had slipped a ring on it.

"Oh, my Lawd," said the reverend, looking down in horror. For there *was* a ring down there, a white metal band, but surrounding the band was his own blood, a thin line. His desire disappeared like a yoyo coming back to the hand that launched it, but the white metal ring closed down to the size of his diminishing desire. And the blood was still there.

"Don't worry, Reverend, that's just a little blood. Do you want to see more?"

And then there was pain in that most delicate place. Reverend Wadson looked down in horror at the growing red drippings.

He grabbed the ring but could not tug it off without tearing his flesh.

"Ah kill you," bellowed the massive man.

"And you lose it, sweety," said Ingrid and she held up a little black box the size of a box of restaurant souvenir matches. It had a small red plastic toggle switch set in the center. She moved the switch forward and the pain in his groin eased. She moved it back and it felt as if someone were sticking pins in a circle around his organ.

"Close up your pants, Reverend. We're going out."

"S'right. Ah gots speech to make. Yessuh, black is beauty. De mos' beautiful. Got to get on wif it right now. Racism, it doan sleep. No suh. Black, it you basic beauty."

"Can the crap, Reverend. You're coming with me."

"Ah's bleeding," wailed Wadson.

"Don't worry. You'll live."

Wadson's big brown eyes looked at the blond woman with distrust.

"C'mon, I didn't go to this trouble to mug you, Reverend."

Reverend Wadson stuffed a used Kleenex around the metallic ring that bound him like a slave. He hoped that it might loosen and with a jerk he could get it off. But it did not loosen and he realized that the little box she held was stronger than a gun. There was some sort of radio wave the box operated on that made the ring smaller or larger. If he were to get a wall between him and that thing, why, the ring might slip off easily.

"If radio contact is broken," said the blond, "you lose everything. The ring closes for good and goodbye your preaching instrument."

Reverend Wadson smiled and handed over his pearl-handled revolver, handle first. He made sure he was always near her as they left the hotel. But not too close. Whenever his big brown hammy paws got near the instrument Ingrid carried, he felt a stinging pain in a most painful place.

They got into Ingrid's car. She drove and told him to get into the back seat where he sat with his hands hovering over his groin. It dawned on him that this was the first waking moment of his adult life that he was with a beautiful woman without organizing some program to get himself into her pants.

Chapter Seven

The building was only three blocks from Macy's in the center of Manhattan but when Macy's and Gimbel's rang their closing bells, the whole area cleared out as if it were a blackboard and God had wiped the wet eraser of night over it.

Reverend Wadson slumped deeper into the back seat of the car as it pulled to a stop in front of an old lime-stained brick building that looked like a hiring hall for rats. He looked cautiously out his side window, then craned his neck to look behind the car.

"Ah doan laks dis place," he said. "This neighborhood not safe dis time of night."

"I'll protect you, Porkchop," Ingrid said.

"Ain' got my piece," said Wadson. "Ain' nobody got no right make somebody go into some place like dis without him got a piece to protects him."

"Like those old white people you turned loose in that jungle tonight? That got burned alive?"

"Weren't my fault," Reverend Wadson said. If he could just get her talking, maybe he could get his hands on that little black box she kept pressed between her legs as she drove. "Dey volunteers. Dey volunteer to make up fo' centuries of white oppression."

Ingrid carefully took off her driving gloves. She seemed in no hurry to leave the car, as if she were waiting for a signal. Wadson moved up slightly on the edge of the seat. One big hand around her neck and her own hands would probably fly up to her throat to save herself. Then he could pluck that little black box from between her legs. But carefully. Carefully.

"They were poor old people who didn't know any better," Ingrid said. "They believed all that bilge that they heard from fakers like you and others just like you. You should have protected them."

"Not my job to give dem protection. Gubbermint not give me 'nough money to give de protection. Gubbermint cheat de black man again and now try to blame dat accident on the black man. Oh, when will it end, dis oppression?" he moaned.

"The strong have an obligation to protect the weak," said Ingrid. "In the old colonies of the western world, that used to be called the white man's burden. Nowadays, in these jungles ..." she paused and started to turn toward him "... it's the jungle bunny's burden."

Wadson had almost reached the edge of his seat when Ingrid turned and gave him a full bright smile of perfect pearlescent teeth. "You move another inch toward me, darkie, and you're going to be singing soprano for the rest of your life."

Reverend Wadson slumped back in the corner of the seat again.

"Ah still doan lak dis place," he said.

"If we're attacked by a marauding band, you can give

102

them all your all-men-are-brothers sermon. That should raise their consciousness. Assuming they have any."

She seemed satisfied that Wadson had given up any aggressive plans, so she turned back and continued looking out the front window. Just to remind him, she touched the red toggle switch atop the black box.

"All right, all right," Wadson said hurriedly then groaned in relief as the pressure was relieved slightly.

The pain was bearable but it was always there. Wadson didn't trust that Ingrid not to mess with that switch so he sat still. Very still. His day would come. One day, he'd get her and she wouldn't have that little black box and he would have his gun and he would do his number on her and then when he was all done, he would turn her over to the Saxon Lords for a toy and they would teach her not to mess with the black man, not to subjugate him and his nobility to her own. . . .

Someone was coming down the street. Three men moved along toward them. Black men. Young black men with big floppy hats and platform shoes and skin-tight trousers. Was that who she was waiting for?

The three men stopped ten feet from the car, peering through the windshield. One bent closer for a better look, saw Ingrid's white blond hair, and pointed toward her. The other two bent over for a better look. They smiled, bright sunshine smiles in their midnight faces. Hitching up their trousers, they sauntered over to the car.

Go 'way, Reverend Wadson thought. Go 'way, we don' want no trouble wif you. But he said nothing.

The biggest of the three young men, who looked to be eighteen years old, tapped on the window near Ingrid's left ear.

She looked at him coolly, then rolled the window down two inches.

"Yes?"

"You lost, lady? We help you if you is lost."

"I'm not lost, thank you."

"Then why you waiting here? Hah. Why you here?"

"I like it here."

"You waiting for a man, you doan have to waits no mo'. Now you gots three mens."

"Wonderful," Ingrid said. "Why don't we all make a date to meet sometime at the monkey house at the zoo?"

"Doan have to wait for no dates to meet wif us. We heah now and we ready for you." He turned to his two companions. "Ain' we ready for her?"

One nodded. The other said, "Oooooh, is we ever?"

"It's been nice talking to you boys. Good night," Ingrid said.

"Wait a minute. Ain' no boys you talking to. No boys. We's men. Where you getting that boys? You doan go doing no boying around heah. We's men. You want to see how big mens we is, we shows you."

He reached down to unzip his fly.

"Take it out and I'll take it off," Ingrid said.

"Take it out," said one of the other youths.

"Yeah. Take it out," said the other. "She 'fraid your black power. Show her your tower of power."

The first youth was confused now. He looked at Ingrid.

"Yo wanna see it?"

"No," she said. "I want your lips. I want your big beautiful lips to kiss."

The boy swelled up and smirked at his two friends. "Well, little foxy lady, ain' no trouble wiffen dat dere." He bent over and put his face toward the car. He puckered his lips in the two-inch opening at the top of the window.

Ingrid stuck Reverend Wadson's pearl-handled revolver into the big open mouth.

"Here, Sambo, suck on this for a while."

The young black man recoiled. "Sheeit," he said.

"Nice to meet you. My name's Ingrid."

"Dis bitch crazy," said the man, wiping the taste of the gun barrel from his mouth.

"This what?" Ingrid asked, pointing the barrel of the gun at the man's stomach.

"Ah sorry. Lady. Come on, boys, we go now. Yes'm, we go now."

"Have a nice day, nigger," Ingrid said.

She pointed the gun at him again as he moved back a step.

"Yes'm," he said. "Yes'm." He put an arm around the shoulder of one of his friends and moved quickly away from the car, careful to make sure that his friend was between him and the gun barrel.

Ingrid rolled up the window. Reverend Wadson breathed again. They had never seen him, hidden in the dark corner of the rear seat. Ingrid seemed content not to talk and Wadson decided not to try to get her to change her mind.

They waited in silence another ten minutes before Ingrid said, "All right. We can go up now." As Reverend Wadson got out of the car, she said, "Lock it up. Your friends may come back and eat the seats if you don't." She waited, then nodded to Wadson to lead the way down the street. She followed, her fingers on the red toggle switch of the little black box.

"Up here," she ordered as they passed in front of a three-story stone tenement. Wadson led the way up to the top floor. There was only one door on the floor and Ingrid pushed Wadson through it, into a large, spartan apartment where Tony Spesk, né Colonel Speskaya, sat on a brown flowered sofa, reading *Commentary Magazine* with a thin smile on his pale face.

He nodded to Ingrid as she entered, and told Wadson to sit down in the chair facing the couch.

"You are here, Reverend Wadson, because we need your services."

"Who you?" Wadson asked.

Spesk grinned, a large wide smile. "We are the people who control your life. That's all you need to know."

With a sudden flash of inspiration, Wadson asked "You communists?"

"You might say that," said Spesk.

"Ah communist too," said Wadson.

"Oh, really?"

"Yeah. Ah believes in share and share alike. Equality Nobody being rich ober de bodies ob de poor. Ah believes in dat."

"How droll," said Spesk. He stood up from the couch carefully placing the magazine on one of the arms. "And what is your viewpoint of the Hegelian dichotomy?"

"Hah?" said Reverend Wadson.

"What do you think of the revolt of the sailors a Kronstadt?" Spesk asked. "The Menshevik heresy?"

"Hah?"

"Of course, you support the labor theory of value a modified by the research of Belchov?"

"Hah?"

"I hope, Reverend Wadson," Spesk said, "that you live to see the Communist victory. Because two day later, you'll be in a field picking cotton. Ingrid, call and make sure our other visitor is on his way."

Ingrid nodded and went from the large living room into a smaller room, closing the door behind her. Wadson noticed that she had placed the small black box on the arm of the couch near Spesk. His chance at last. An opening.

When the door had closed behind Ingrid, he smiled a Spesk.

"That one bad woman."

"Oh?" said Spesk.

"Yeah. She a racist. She hate black men. She commiting a 'trocity on me."

"Too bad, Wadson. Next to me, she looks like Albert chweitzer."

His eyes had a strange hard glint in them and while Reverend Wadson didn't know who Albert Schweitzer was, because he didn't pay too much attention to the omings and goings of Jews, he decided Spesk's comment retty well sealed off the prospect of a counterconspiracy against Ingrid. And the black box was still too far way.

"Listen, Mister . . ."

"Spesk. Tony Spesk."

"Well, listen Mr. Spesk, she got dis ring on me and it urts. You fixing to let me loose?"

"A day or two if you behave yourself. Never, if you ause me any trouble."

"I causes you no trouble," Wadson said. "I be the east troubling man you ever likely to find."

"Good, because I need you for something. Sit on the oor and listen."

Wadson moved off the chair and lowered himself to he floor, carefully, as if he had raw eggs in his back ockets.

"There is a white man. He travels with an old Orienal. I want them."

"You gots dem. Where is they?"

"I don't know. I saw them down in your neighborood. Near the house where that old woman, Mrs. ueller, was killed."

Mrs. Mueller? Mrs. Mueller? That was the old woman e government was so interested in. They had been oking for something. And whatever it was Wadson had . Her apartment had yielded only junk, but there was strange-looking device that the Saxon Lords had rought Wadson to try to fence.

107

"I gots something better dan any white man an chink," Wadson said.

"What is that?"

"Dey was dis thing that the Missus Mueller had an the government, it was lookin' for."

"Yes."

"I got de ting."

"What is it?" Spesk said.

"Ah doan know. It some kind of ting that goes tic and tick, but ah doan knows what it's for."

"Where do you have it?"

"You takes de ring off, I tell you." Wadson tried large friendly smile.

"You don't tell me and I'm going to take part of yo off." Spesk reached out and lifted the small black box.

"Hold it, hold it, hold it raht theah. I got the de vice. I got it at my 'partment."

"Good. I want it. But more than that, I want th white man and the Oriental."

"I find dem. I get dem for you. What you want de for?"

"They're weapons. Never mind. You wouldn't unde stand."

"You gonna take de ring off?"

"When you perform."

Wadson nodded glumly. Spesk took several steps bac to the couch. He was limping heavily.

"What happen to you leg?"

"That's what I want to see the white man about Spesk said.

"What white man?"

"What have we been talking about? The white ma and the Oriental."

"Oh, dat white man."

Spesk looked up as Ingrid returned.

"I just saw his car. He's on his way up," she said.

"Fine. You know what to do."

Though the wood parquet floor was hard under Reverend Wadson's butt he didn't think it would be wise to move. That black box was still too close to Spesk's hand. He sat still as Ingrid went back into the other room and came out with another black box. She gave it to Spesk. She was also carrying a hoop, a round white ring of metal, the size of a hoop from a child's ring-toss game.

Spesk held the black box in his hands and nodded to Ingrid who walked to the door of the apartment and stood behind the door.

A few seconds later, the door opened, and a small man with a graying crew cut splashed into the room. He came at top speed as if he had just remembered where he had misplaced his wallet. He looked up and saw Spesk and smiled.

The man paused a moment, as if psychically recharging himself for another frenzied bolt across the floor toward Spesk, when Ingrid stepped from behind the door and with one quick practiced motion opened the white ring and snapped it around the man's neck.

The man recoiled and spun toward her, his right hand slipping immediately into the jacket of his plaid sports jacket.

"Breslau," Spesk said. His voice, uttering one word, was a harsh command demanding obedience. Breslau turned. He put his hands to the ring on his neck and tried to pull it off. When it did not come loose, he looked at Spesk and his smile was gone. His face was all questions.

"Leave that alone and come here," Spesk said.

The small man looked at Ingrid once more as if filing her perfidy for a future accounting date, then came toward Spesk. He finally saw Reverend Wadson on the floor and looked at him, unsure whether to smile in welcome or to sneer in victory. Instead he just looked blankly at Wadson, and then again at Spesk.

"Colonel Speskaya," Breslau said. "I heard you were in the city. I could not wait to talk to you." His hands again went to the ring at his neck. "But what is this? Most strange." He smiled at Spesk as if they alone in the world shared a secret knowledge of the earth's grossest stupidities.

He glanced at Wadson to see if the black man had a similar ring around his neck. Wadson wanted to shout, "Honkey, I gots one worse than that."

"Breslau," Spesk said coldly. "You know a house on Walton Avenue?"

The small smile of secret sharing left Breslau's face but only for an instant before he recovered. "But of course, Colonel. That is why I was most anxious to see you. To discuss this with you."

"And that is why you and your superiors saw fit not to notify us of what you were doing and what you were looking for?"

"It might have been a fruitless search," Breslau said. "It was, in fact. I would not want to bother you with trivia."

Spesk looked down at the small black box in his hands.

"I will give you some trivia," he said. "You did not notify us because your agency was freelancing again and trying to capture this device for yourself. East Germany has always had such ambitions." He raised a hand to silence Breslau's protest. "You were awkward and inept. There would have been ways to move into that building, to search for something of value. We could simply have bought the building through a front. But, no, that would have been too simple. So you had to blunder around and finally bring in the American CIA and the

110

merican FBI and they took the operation away from
ou."

Breslau did not know yet if it was the right time to
rotest. His face seemed frozen.

"Ineptitude is bad enough," Spesk said. "Ineptitude
at results in failure is even worse. It is intolerable.
ou may speak now."

"You are right, Comrade. We should have advised you
arlier. But as I say, the device was only a rumor among
ome of those in the German Democratic Republic who
ere active during the war. It could well have been only
figment of someone's imagination. As in fact it was.
here is no such device."

"Wrong. There is."

"There is?" Breslau's suprise had overtones of sadness.

"Yes. This creature has it. He is going to give it to
e."

Breslau looked at Wadson again. "Well, that's wonder-
l. Marvelous."

"Isn't it?" Spesk said drily, rejecting the partnership
at Breslau had tried to construct with his tone of
oice.

"And this device, is it of value? Will we be able to use
in the future in the battle against the imperialists?"

"I have not seen it," Spesk said. "But it is a device.
here are devices and devices." Finally Wadson saw him
mile. "Like the thing around your neck."

"Is this it?" Breslau said. His hands went to the ring
round his throat.

"No. That is something new we have just invented. I
ill show you how it works."

As Wadson watched, Spesk pushed forward the red
oggle switch on the small black box. Breslau gagged.
Iis eyes bulged.

"*Aaaaggghhh.*" His hands clawed at the ring.

111

"You are being removed, Comrade," said Spesk, "not because you have been deceitful but because you have been caught at it. Too bad."

He pushed the switch forward farther, a mere fraction of an inch. Breslau dropped to his knees. His fingertips dug into his neck in an effort to make room for his fingers behind the tightening white ring. Where his fingernails dug, they left trails of blood on his throat as they gouged out skin and flesh. Wadson felt a sympathetic pain in his groin.

Breslau's mouth opened. His eyes bulged out farther, like a man who spent a year on a diet of thyroid extract.

"Enjoy, enjoy," Spesk said. He pushed the switch all the way forward. There was a crack that sounded like a wooden pencil being broken. Breslau fell face forward onto the floor with a final hiss of air from his lungs, that turned into a small red bubbly froth leaking out of the corner of his mouth. His eyes stared at Reverend Wadson and already, the black man could see them begin to haze over.

Wadson grimaced.

"You," Spesk said. He put down the one black box and picked up the other. "You know now what I want you to do."

"Yassuh," said Wadson.

"Repeat it."

"Yo' wants me to find dis white man and dis yellow man and den brings dem here." He rolled his eyes and smiled a big pancake. "Dat it, boss?"

"Yes. There will be no mistakes?"

"No 'stakes. Nossuh, Missah Tony."

"Good. You may leave now. Ingrid will go with you to keep an eye on you and to examine this device that came from the Mueller apartment. I warn you. Do not be foolish and try to attack Ingrid. She is a very good agent."

Wadson got to his feet slowly and quietly, lest a heavily placed heel infuriate Spesk and he begin playing with that red toggle switch. The reverend turned to look for Ingrid. She was standing behind him, looking down at the dead body of East German agent Breslau.

And her nipples were hard again, Wadson noticed. And he wished they weren't.

Chapter Eight

Two bath towels were bunched up at one end of the tub but the newspapers Remo had spread on the floor were still dry and he felt like patting Tyrone's head when he unlocked the bathroom door and let him out.

Tyrone ran immediately for the front door of the hotel suite. His hand was on the doorknob when he felt himself being jerked backward, up into the air, and plummeting down onto a couch which exhaled air with an asthmatic whoosh when Tyrone's 147 pounds landed on it.

"What's the big hurry?" Remo said.

"Ah wants get outta here."

"You see," Chiun said, standing near the window and looking out toward Central Park. "He wants. Therefore it must be done now. Instant gratification. How typical of the young."

"Except for the way it's piled, this garbage isn't typical of anything, Little Father."

114

"Yo' better lets me go now. Ah gotta go," Tyrone said. "Ah wants to be leavin'."

"You wants, you wants," Remo said. "What do you deserveses?"

"Ah gots go school."

"School? You?"

"Assright. And ah gots go or ah gets in trouble and yo' be in trouble 'cause it's de law dat ah go school."

"Little Father," Remo asked, "what could they teach his thing in school? They've had him most of his life already and they still haven't been able to teach him English."

"Maybe it is an intelligent school system," Chiun said, "and devotes no time to the study of inferior languages."

"No," said Remo. "I can't believe that."

"Dey teach me," said Tyrone, "and ah learns. Ah peaks street English. Dat de real English before it be robbed by de white man who ruin it when he steal it from de black man."

"Where'd you hear that drivel?" Remo asked.

"Ah hears it in de school. Dey have dis man who write de book and he tell us that we talk real fine and everybody else, dey be wrong. He say we speak de real English."

"Listen to this, Chiun. You don't have to like English but it's my language. It's a shame to hear this done to it." Remo turned to Tyrone again. "This man who wrote that book about your English. Is he in your school?"

"Yeah. He de guidance counsellor at Malcolm-King-Lumumba. He one smart muvver."

"Remember what I told you last night?" Remo asked.

" 'Bout killing me?"

Remo nodded. "I haven't made up my mind yet. If I find out you're responsible for you, then you're going to vanish without leaving a spot. But if it's not your fault,

115

then, well maybe, just maybe, you'll live. Come on
We're going to talk to your guidance counselor. On you
feet, Tyrone."

"Those are the things at the ends of your legs," Chiur
said.

The Malcolm-King-Lumumba School had cost nine
teen million dollars when it had been built five year
earlier. The building covered one square block, and th
interior of the building surrounded a central court o
walkways, picnic tables, and outdoor basketball back
boards.

When the city had first designed the building, the na
tionally famous architect had called for a minimum o
glasswork along the four exterior sides of the building
This would be compensated by window walls on the in
side of the building, bordering the courtyard.

The community school board had attacked the plan
as racist attempts to hide away black children. A publi
relations firm hired by the school board mounted a cam
paign whose theme was "What do they have to hide?"
and "Bring the schools out into the light" and "Don'
send our children back to the cave."

The New York City central school board surrendered
to community pressure in forty-eight hours. The school'
plans were redrawn. The inside of the school buildin
still had floor-to-ceiling windows, but the perimeter o
Malcolm-King-Lumumba was changed from mostl
stone to mostly glass.

The first year, the cost of replacing broken glas
caused by passing rock tossers was $140,000; the secon
year, new glass cost $231,000. In four years, the cost o
windows for Malcolm-King-Lumumba exceeded one mil
lion dollars.

In the fifth year, two important things happened. Th
city faced a budget crunch in the schools. When th
budget cut hit Lumumba High, the president of th

community school board knew just where to cut expenses, because of the second important thing: his brother, having been made almost a millionaire by four years of supplying windows to the school, sold his glass business and opened a lumberyard.

Lumumba High stopped replacing glass. They boarded up all the big window openings around the four outside walls of the school with plywood. The first year's cost was $63,000.

Lumumba High was now sealed off from the outside world by a wall of stone and exterior-grade Douglas fir plywood through which not light or air or learning could penetrate.

When a member of the community school board protested about the plywood and the resultant lack of light and asked a meeting "What are they trying to hide?" and to "Let our children out of the dark," he was beaten up on his way home after the meeting. There had been no protests since that time.

When the architect who had originally designed the school drove up one day to look at it, he sat in his car for an hour weeping.

Remo deposited Tyrone Walker inside the main corridor of Malcolm-King-Lumumba School.

"Now you go to your classes," Remo said.

Tyrone nodded but looked toward the front door where a pale knife-edge of sunlight slipped in alongside one of the plywood panels.

"No, Tyrone," said Remo. "You go to your classes. If you don't and you try to get away, I'll come and find you. And you won't like that."

Tyrone nodded again, glumly. He swallowed with a gulp as if trying to devour a swollen gland in his throat.

"And don't you leave here without me," Remo said.

"What' yo do?"

"I'm going to talk to some of the people here and see if it's your fault or theirs that you are what you are."

"All right, all right," said Tyrone. "Anyways, dis nice day to be in school. We gots de reading today."

"You study reading? I thought you didn't." Remo was impressed.

"Well, not dat honkey kind of shit. De teacher, she read to us."

"What's she read?"

"Outen a big book wifout de pitchers."

"Get out of here, Tyrone," Remo said.

After Tyrone left, Remo looked around for the office. Two young men who looked to be ten years older than the minimum age for quitting school walked toward him and Remo asked if they knew where the office was.

"You got a nickel, man?" said one.

"Actually, no," Remo said. "But I've got cash. Probably two thousand, three thousand dollars. I don't like to walk around broke."

"Den you gives us some bread iffen you wants de office."

"Go surround a ham hock," Remo said.

The young man backed off a step from Remo, and with a jerking movement of his hand, had a switchblade out of his pocket and aimed at Remo's belly.

"Now you gives us bread."

The other young man stood off to the side, applauding quietly, a big smile on his face.

"You know," Remo said, "school is a great learning experience."

The man with the knife looked confused. "Ah doan wanna . . ."

"For instance," Remo said, "you're going to learn what it feels like to have your wrist bones mashed to jelly."

The knife wavered in the hand of the young man.

Remo moved a step closer and as if responding to a dare, the youth pushed the blade forward. The first thing he heard was the click as the knife blade hit the stone floor. The next thing he heard was a series of clicks as the bones were shattering in his right wrist, in the twisting grip of the white man.

The man opened his mouth to scream, but Remo clamped a hand over his face.

"Mustn't make loud noises. You'll disrupt the little scholars at their work. Now where's the office?"

He looked at the second young man who said, "Down that corridor. First door on the right."

"Thank you," Remo said. "Nice talking to you boys."

The door to the office was solid steel without windows and Remo had to lean his weight on it before it pushed open.

Remo walked up to the long counter inside the office and waited. Finally a woman appeared and asked "Wha' yo' want?" The woman was tall and overweight, her hair a haloed mountain of frizz around her head.

An office door to Remo's left said, "Doctor Shockley, Guidance Counselor."

"I want to see him," Remo said, pointing toward the door.

"Him's busy. What yo' want see him 'bout?"

"One of your students. A Tyrone Walker."

"De police precinct be down de street. Tell dem 'bout dis Tyrone."

"I'm not here with a police problem. I want to talk about Tyrone's schoolwork."

"Who you?"

"I'm a friend of the family. Tyrone's parents are both working today and they asked me to stop by and see what I could do."

"Wha' yo' say?" The woman's eyes narrowed suspiciously.

"I thought I was speaking English. Tyrone's folks are working and they wanted me . . ."

"Ah hear you. Ah hear you. What kind of silly story be dat? What kind of people you tink we is, you come in and try to fool us like dat?"

"Fool you?" asked Remo.

"Nobody gots no folks what bofe be working. Why you heah tellin' dem lies?"

Remo sighed. "I don't know why I bother. All right. I'm Tyrone's parole officer. I think he's violated parole with a triple rape and six murders. I want to talk to Shockley before I send him to the electric chair."

"Dat better, you be tellin' de troof now. You sit down and you wait and Shockley be wif you when he gets chancet. He busy."

The woman nodded Remo toward a chair and went back to her desk and a copy of *Essential Magazine, the Journal of Black Beauty*. She stared at the cover.

Remo found himself sitting next to a teenage boy who was staring hard at a coloring book on his lap. It was open to a cartoon of Porky Pig sniffing a flower in front of a barn.

The boy took a crayon from his shirt pocket, colored one of Porky's fat round hams pink, then replaced the crayon. He took out a green one and colored the roof of the barn. He replaced that crayon and took out the pink one again to do Porky's other rear leg.

Remo watched over the boy's shoulder.

"You're pretty good," he said.

"Yeah, I do de best in de art appreciation classes."

"I can see why. You almost stay inside all the lines."

"Sometime it be hard though when de lines close together and de point of de crayon don't fit 'tween dem."

"What do you do then?" asked Remo.

"Ah takes a crayon from somebody whats got a sharp one and ah use dat one to fit in 'tween de lines."

"And you give him your old crayon?"

The boy looked at Remo, a look of confusion on his face as if Remo were speaking a language he had never heard.

"Whuffo ah do that? Ah trows de old crayon away. You a social worker or somefin?"

"No, but sometimes I wish I were."

"Yo' talks funny. 'If ah were' you says."

"That's called English."

"Yeah. That. What your name?"

"Bwana Sahib," Remo said.

"You son of great Arab chief too?"

"I'm a direct descendant of that great Arabian chief, Pocahontas."

"Great Arab chiefs, dey be black," the boy sniffed. He knew a fool when he saw one.

"I was on his mother's side," Remo said. "Go back to coloring."

"It all right. Ah gots till tomorra to finish it."

Remo shook his head. At the desk, the black woman was still staring at the cover of *Essential Magazine, the Journal of Black Beauty.*

Shockley's office door opened slightly and Remo heard a voice.

"Rat bastard," came a shriek. "You be discriminating. Dat not be fair."

The door opened fully and a woman stood in the opening, her back to Remo. She was shaking a fist at something inside the room. The woman had big thick hams that jiggled below the flowered belt of her cotton dress. Her hips looked like a hassock with a bite taken out of it. Her flailing arms set off wave movements in the oceans of fat that hung from her upper biceps.

A voice inside the room said something softly.

"You still a rat bastard," she said. "If you didn't have dat, I show you a ting or two."

She turned and stepped toward Remo. If hate had been electricity, her eyes would have sparked. Her lips were pressed tight together and her nostrils flared.

For a moment, Remo considered running lest the mastodon get her hands on him. But she stopped next to the boy who was coloring.

"Come on, Shabazz, we going home."

The boy was trying to finish up the coloring of Porky Pig's right front leg. Remo could hear his teeth grind as he concentrated. The woman lingered only for a moment, then clubbed the boy alongside the head. Crayon went flying one way, the coloring book the other.

"Come on, ma, why you do dat?"

"We gettin' outta here. Dat rat bastard, he not gonna change his mind 'bout you graduating."

"You mean your son here is not going to be graduated?" Remo said. "He's going to be left back?" Maybe there was still some sanity in the world.

The woman looked at Remo as if he were a fried rib that had lain all night on a subway platform.

"What you talking? Shabazz here, he de salitate-atorian. He got honors."

"Then what's the problem?" Remo asked.

"De problem is Shabazz gots go away on May fif-teempf. And dat no good Shockley, he won't change de graduation and make it no earlier so dat Shabazz get his diploma before he go to de jail. He do de five years for de robbery."

"That must be heartbreaking after Shabazz works so hard coloring inside the lines."

"Dat right," said the mother. "C'mon, Shabazz, we gets outta dis motherfuckin' place."

Shabazz shuffled to his feet. The sixteen-year-old was taller than Remo. Standing next to his mother, he looked like a pencil leaning against a pencil sharpener.

He followed the woman from the room, leaving his

crayon and coloring book on the floor where she had knocked them. Remo picked them up and put them on the small end table that held a lamp, bolted to the table with long steel stove bolts.

Remo looked across the counter at the woman who was still staring at the cover of *Essential Magazine, the Journal of Black Beauty,* her big lips moving slowly as if she were trying to crush a very small guppy to death between them. She finally took a deep breath and turned the cover to the front page.

"Excuse, me," Remo said. "May I go in now?"

The woman slammed shut the cover of the magazine. "Sheeit," she said. "Always inneruptions. Now ah got to start all over 'gain."

"I won't bother you again," Remo said. "I'll be quiet."

"You do that, heah? Go 'head in, iffen you wants."

Doctor Shockley's office was really two offices. There was the part Remo stood in, just inside the door, a skeleton of a room with three chairs bolted to the vinyl-tiled floor and a lamp that was riveted to the floor and had a tamperproof wire screen around the bare bulb.

The other part of the office was where Shockley sat at a desk. Behind him were shelves filled with books, tape recorders, and statues of African artifacts that were made in a small town in Illinois. And between the two halves of the office was a screen, a tight steel mesh that ran from wall to floor, from floor to ceiling, effectively separating Shockley from anyone who might come into his office. Next to his desk, a gate was built into the screen. It was fastened on Shockley's side with a heavy bulletproof padlock.

Shockley was a trim black man with a modest Afro and darting eyes. He wore a pin-striped gray suit with a pink shirt and black figured tie. His fingernails were manicured, Remo noticed, and he wore a thin gold Omega watch on his narrow wrist.

His hands were open on his desk, palm side down. Next to his right hand was a .357 Magnum. Remo had to look twice before he believed it. The gun had notches on the carved wooden grip.

Shockley smiled at Remo as Remo approached the screen.

"Won't you sit down, please?" His voice was nasal, bored, and precise, the adenoidal Ivy League squeak that clips off words as if they are unworthy to remain in the speaker's mouth.

"Thank you," Remo said.

"What may I do for you?" Shockley asked.

"I'm a friend of the family. I've come to inquire about one of your students. A Tyrone Walker."

"Tyrone Walker? Tyrone Walker? Just a moment."

Shockley pressed a panel built into his desk and a television monitor popped up from inside the left edge of the desk. He pressed some buttons on a typewriter keyboard and Remo could see the reflection in his eyes as a flicker of light illuminated the screen.

"Oh yes. Tyrone Walker." Shockley looked toward Remo with a smile of love and beneficence. "You'll be happy to know, Mr. . . . Mister?"

"Sahib," Remo said. "Bwana Sahib."

"Well, Mr. Sahib, you'll be happy to know that Tyrone is doing just fine."

"I beg your pardon," Remo said.

"Tyrone Walker is doing just fine."

"Tyrone Walker is a living time bomb," Remo said. "It is just a matter of when he explodes and hurts someone. He is a functional illiterate, barely housebroken. How can he be doing fine?"

As he spoke, Remo had started to come up out of his

chair and Shockley's hand moved slowly toward the Magnum. He relaxed as Remo sat back in the seat.

"It's all right here, Mr. Sahib. And computers never lie. Tyrone is at the top of his class in language arts, near the top in word graphic presentation, and in the top twentieth percentile in basic computational skills."

"Let me guess," Remo said. "That's reading, writing, and arithmetic."

Shockley smiled a small smile. "Well, in the old days, it was called that. Before we moved into new relevant areas of education."

"Name one," Remo said.

"It's all right here in one of my books," Shockley said. He waved his left hand toward a shelf of books directly behind his left shoulder. *"Adventures in Education—An Answer to the Question of Racism in the Classroom."*

"You wrote that?" Remo asked.

"I've written all these books, Mr. Sahib," Shockley said. *"Racism on Trial, Inequality in the Classroom, The Black Cultural Experience and its Effect on Learning, Street English—A Historical Imperative."*

"Have you written anything about how to teach kids to read and write?"

"Yes. My masterwork is considered *Street English, A Historial Imperative.* It tells how the true English was the black man's English and the white power structure changed it into something it was never meant to be, thereby setting ghetto children at a disadvantage."

"That's idiotic," Remo said.

"Is it? Did you know that the word 'algebra' is itself an Arabic word? And the Arabs are, of course, black."

"They'd be interested in hearing that," Remo said. "What's your answer to this disadvantage of ghetto children in learning English?"

"Let us return to the true basic form of English, Street English. Black English, if you will."

"In other words, because these bunnies can't talk right, make their stupidity the standard by which you judge everybody else?"

"That is racist, Mr. Sahib," Shockley said indignantly.

"I notice you don't speak this Street English," Remo said. "If it's so pure, why don't you?"

"I have my educational doctorate from Harvard," Shockley said. His nostrils pinched tighter together as he said it.

"That's no answer. Are you saying you don't speak Street English because you're smart enough not to?"

"Street English is quite capable of being understood on the streets."

"What if they want to get off the streets? What if they need to know something more than 127 different ways to shake hands? What happens when they go into the real world where most people talk real English? They'll sound as stupid and backward as that clerk of yours out there." Remo waved toward the door, outside which he could still imagine the woman sitting at the desk, worrying to death the seven words on the cover of *Essential Magazine, the Journal of Black Beauty.*

"Clerk?" said Shockley. His eyes raised in a pair of question marks.

"Yes. That woman out there."

Shockley chuckled. "Oh. You must mean Doctor Bengazi."

"No, I don't mean Doctor anybody. I mean that woman out there who can't read."

"Tall woman?"

Remo nodded.

"Big frizzy do?" Shockley surrounded his hair with his hands.

Remo nodded.

Shockley nodded back. "Doctor Bengazi. Our principal."

"God help us all."

Remo and Shockley looked at each other for long seconds without speaking.

Finally Remo said, "Seeing as how nobody wants to teach these kids to read or write, why not teach them trades? To be plumbers or carpenters or truckdrivers or something."

"How quick you all are to consign these children to the scrap heap. Why should they not have a full opportunity to share in the riches of American life?"

"Then why the hell don't you prepare them for that full opportunity?" Remo asked. "Teach them to read, for Christ's sake. You ever leave a kid back?"

"Leave a child back? What does that mean?"

"You know. Fail to promote him because his work isn't good enough."

"We have done away with those vestigial traces of racism. IQ tests, examinations, report cards, promotions. Every child advances with his or her peer group, socially adept, with the basic skills of community interaction attuned to the higher meaning of the ethnic experience."

"But they can't read," Remo yelled.

"I think you overstate the case somewhat," Shockley said, with the satisfied smile of a man trying to impress the drunken stranger on the next bar stool.

"I just saw your salutatorian. He can't even color inside the lines."

"Shabazz is a very bright boy. He has indigenous advancement attitudes."

"He's a frigging armed robber."

"To err is human. To forgive divine," Shockley said.

"Why didn't you forgive him then and change the date of graduation for him?" Remo asked.

"I couldn't. I just changed it to another date and I couldn't make any more changes."

"Why'd you change it the first time?"

"For the valedictorian."

"What's he going up for?" Remo asked.

"It is a she, Mr. Sahib. And no, she is not going to jail. However, she is going to enjoy the meaningful experience of giving birth."

"And you moved up the graduation so she wouldn't foal on the stage?"

"That's crude," Shockley said.

"Did you ever think, Mr. Shockley . . ."

"Doctor Shockley. Doctor."

"Did you ever think, Doctor Shockley, that perhaps it's your policies that reduce you to this?"

"To what?"

"To sitting here, barricaded in your office behind a metal fence, a gun in your hand. Did it ever occur to you that if you treated your kids as humans, with rights and responsibilities, they might act like humans?"

"And you think I could do this by 'leaving them back,' as you so quaintly put it?"

"For a start, yeah. Maybe if the others see that they've got to work, they'll work. Demand something from them."

"By leaving them back? Now I'll give you an example. Each September, we take one hundred children into the first grade. Now suppose I was to leave back all one hundred because they were unable to perform satisfactorily on some arbitrary test of learning experience . . ."

"Like going to the bathroom," Remo interrupted.

"If I were to leave back all hundred, then next September I would have two hundred children in the first grade and the September after that, three hundred children. It would never stop and after a few years I would be running a school in which everyone was in the first grade."

Remo shook his head. "That presupposes that all of

128

them would be left back. You really don't believe that these kids can be taught to read or write, do you?"

"They can be taught the beauty of black culture, the richness of their experience in America, and how they overcame degradation and the white man's slavery, they can be taught . . ."

"You don't believe that they can be taught to learn anything," Remo said again. He stood up. "Shockley, you're a racist, you know that? You're the worst racist I ever met. You'll accept anything, any garbage, from these kids because you don't think they're capable of doing any better."

"I? A racist?" Shockley chuckled and pointed to the wall. "There is my award for promoting the ideals of brotherhood, equality, and black excellence, presented to me on behalf of a grateful community by the Black Ministry Council. So much for racism."

"Where does that computer say Tyrone is now?"

Shockley checked the small screen, then punched another button on its keyboard. "Room 127, Advanced Communications."

"Good," Remo said. "I can just follow the sound of the grunts."

"I'm not sure you understand the new aims of modern education, Mr. Sahib."

"Forget it, pal," Remo said.

"But you . . ."

Suddenly it spilled out of Remo. The agonizing discussion with Shockley, the stupidity of the man who had been put in control of hundreds of young lives, the transparent hypocrisy of a man who thought that if children lived in the gutter, the thing to do was to sanctify the gutter with pious words, all of it filled Remo up like a too-rich meal and he could feel the bile rising in his throat. For the second time in less than twenty-four hours, he lost his temper.

Before Shockley could move, Remo's hand flashed out and ripped a foot-square hole in the steel screen. Shockley's hands groped out, grasping for his .357 Magnum but it wasn't there. It was in the crazy white man's hands, and as Shockley watched in horror, Remo snapped off the barrel just behind the cylinder. He looked at the useless weapon, then tossed both parts onto the desk in front of Shockley.

"There," he said.

Shockley's face was screwed up in anguish as if someone had just squirted ammonia into his nostrils.

"Why you do that?" he whined.

"Just write it off as another indigenous ethnic experience in racist white America," Remo said. "That's a book title. It's yours for free."

Shockley picked up both parts of the pistol and looked at them. Remo thought he was going to cry.

"You shouldna done dat," Shockley said and turned bloodhound eyes on Remo.

Remo shrugged.

"What I go do now?" Shockley asked.

"Write another book. Call it *Racism on the Rampage.*"

"You shouldna done dat ting," Shockley said. "I gots de parents conference all dis appernoon and now whats I gonna do wif no gun?"

"Stop hiding behind that screen like a goddam fireplace log and come out and talk to the parents. Maybe they'll tell you that they'd like their kids to learn to read and write. So long."

Remo walked to the door. He stopped and turned as he heard Shockley mumbling.

"Deys gonna get me. Deys gonna get me. Oh, lawdy, deys gonna get me and me wiffen no gun."

"That's the biz, sweetheart," Remo said.

130

When Remo went to collect Tyrone Walker, he wasn't sure if he had walked into Room 127 or the sixth annual reunion celebration of the Manson Family.

There were twenty-seven black teenagers in the classroom, a limit set by state law because a larger class would have disrupted the learning experience. A half dozen sat round a windowsill in the far corner, passing a hand-rolled cigarette from hand to hand. The room reeked with the deep bitter smell of marijuana. Three tall youths amused themselves by throwing switchblade knives at a picture of Martin Luther King that was Scotch-taped to one of the pecan-paneled walls of the classroom. Most of the students lounged at and on desks, their feet up on other desks, listening to transistor radios that blared forth the top four songs on the week's hit parade, "Love is Stoned," "Stone in Love," "In Love I'm Stoned," and "Don't Stone My Love." The din in the classroom sounded like a half dozen symphony orchestras warming up at the same time. In a bus.

Three very pregnant girls stood by a side wall, talking to each other, giggling and drinking wine from a small pint bottle of muscatel. Remo looked around for Tyrone and found him sleeping across two desks.

Remo drew a few glances from some of the students who then dismissed him with contempt and disdain by turning away.

At the head of the classroom, seated at a desk, bent over a pile of papers, was an iron-haired woman wearing a small-size version of a man's wrist watch and a severe black dress. There was a little nameplate screwed into the teacher's desk. It read Miss Feldman.

The teacher did not look up and Remo stood alongside her desk, watching what she was doing.

She had a stack of sheets of lined paper in front of her. On the top of each sheet was rubber-stamped the name of a student. Most of the papers she looked at were blank, except for the rubber-stamped name. On the blank papers, Miss Feldman marked a neat 90 percent in the upper right hand corner.

An occasional sheet would have some scratched pencil scrawls on it. Those Miss Feldman marked 99 percent with three lines under the score for emphasis and carefully glued a gold star to the top center of the sheet.

She went through a dozen sheets before she realized someone was standing at her desk. She looked up, startled, then relaxed when she saw Remo.

"What are you doing?" he asked.

She smiled at him but said nothing.

"What are you doing?" Remo repeated.

Miss Feldman continued to smile.

No wonder, Remo thought. The teacher was simple. Maybe brain damaged. Then he saw the reason. There were tufts of cotton stuck into Miss Feldman's ears.

Remo reached down and yanked them out. She winced as the rock and roar of the classroom assaulted her eardrums.

"I asked what are you doing?"

"Marking test papers."

"A blank is a 90, a scratch is a 99 with a gold star?" Remo said.

"You must reward effort," Miss Feldman said. She ducked as a book came whizzing by her head, thrown from the back of the room.

"What kind of test?" Remo asked.

"Basic tools of language art," said Miss Feldman.

"Which means?"

"The alphabet."

"You tested them on the alphabet. And most of them turned in blank pages? And they get 90s?"

Miss Feldman smiled. She looked over her shoulder as if someone could sneak up behind her in the three inches she had left between her back and the wall.

"How long have you done this kind of work?" Remo said.

"I've been a teacher for thirty years."

"You've never been a teacher," Remo said. And she hadn't. A teacher was Sister Mary Margaret who knew that while the road to hell was paved with good intentions, the road to heaven was paved with good deeds, hard work, discipline, and a demand for excellence from each student. She had worked in the Newark Orphanage where Remo had grown up and whenever he thought of her, he could almost feel the bruises her ruler raps on the knuckles had given him when she felt he was not trying hard enough.

"What do you make here?" Remo asked.

"Twenty-one thousand, three hundred, and twelve dollars," Miss Feldman answered. Sister Mary Margaret had never seen a hundred dollars at one time in her whole life.

"Why don't you try teaching these kids?" Remo asked.

"You're from the community school board?" Miss Feldman said suspiciously.

"No."

"The central school board?"

"No."

"The financial control board?"

"No."

"The state superintendent's office?"

"No."

"The federal office of education?"

"No. I'm not from nobody. I'm just from me. And I'm wondering why you don't teach these kids anything."

"Just from you?"

"Yes."

"Well, Mister Just-from-You, I've been in this school for eight years. The first week I was here, they tried to rape me three times. The first marking period, I failed two-thirds of the class and the tires were slashed on my car. The second marking period, I failed six kids and my car was set on fire. Next marking period, more failures, and my dog's throat was cut in my apartment while I slept. Then the parents picketed the school, protesting my racist, antiblack attitudes.

"The school board, those paragons of backbone, suspended me for three months. When I came back, I brought a bag of gold stars with me. I haven't had any trouble since and I'm retiring next year. What would you have expected me to do?"

"You could teach," Remo said.

"The essential difference between trying to teach this class and trying to teach a gravel pit is that you can't get raped by a gravel pit," Miss Feldman said. "Rocks don't carry knives."

She looked down at the papers in front of her. One paper had five neat rows of five letters each. Twenty-five letters. Miss Feldman marked it 100 percent with four gold stars.

"The valedictorian?" Remo asked.

"Yes. She always has trouble with the W's."

"If you tried to teach, could they learn?" Remo asked.

"Not by the time they reach me," Miss Feldman said. "This is a senior class. If they're illiterate when they get here, they stay illiterate. They could be taught in the early grades though. If everybody would just realize that giving a failing mark to a black kid doesn't mean that you're a racist who wants to go back to slaveholding. But they have to do it in the early grades."

As Remo watched, a small tear formed in the inside corner of Miss Feldman's left eye.

"And they don't," he said.

"They don't. And so I sit here putting gold stars on papers that twenty years ago would have been grounds for expulsion, black student or white student. What we've come to."

"I'm a friend of Tyrone's. How's he doing?"

"As compared to?"

"The rest of the class," Remo said.

"With luck, he'll go to prison before he's eighteen. That way he'll never starve to death."

"If you had it in your power to decide, would you keep him alive? Would you keep any of them alive?"

"I'd kill them all over the age of six. And I'd start fresh with the young ones and make them work. Make them learn. Make them think."

"Almost like a teacher," Remo said.

She looked up at him sadly. "Almost," she agreed.

Remo turned away and clapped Tyrone on the shoulder. He woke with a start that nearly tipped over the desks.

"Come on, clown," Remo said. "Time to go home."

"Quittin' bell ring already?" Tyrone asked.

Chapter Nine

The fact that Tyrone Watson had made one of his infrequent appearances in class was quickly noted by one Jamie Rickets, alias Ali Muhammid, alias Ibn Faroudi, alias Aga Akbar, AKA Jimmy the Blade.

Jamie talked briefly to Tyrone, then left Malcolm-King-Lumumba School and jumped the wires on the first car he found with an unlocked door and drove the twelve blocks back to Walton Avenue.

In a pool hall, he found the vice counselor of the Saxon Lords and related that Tyrone had mentioned he spent the night at the Hotel Plaza in Manhattan. The vice counselor of the Saxon Lords went to the corner tavern and told the deputy subregent of the Saxon Lords who repeated the message to the deputy minister of war. Actually, the Saxon Lords had no minister of war who would have a deputy. But the title "deputy minister of war," it was decided, was longer and more impressive sounding than minister of war.

136

The deputy minister of war repeated it to the sub-counselor of the Saxon Lords, whom he found sleeping in a burned-out laundromat.

Twenty five minutes later, the subcounselor finally found the Saxon Lords' Leader for Life, sleeping on a bare mattress in the first-floor-left apartment of an abandoned building.

The Leader for Life, who had held the job for less than twelve hours since the sudden schoolyard demise of the last Leader for Life, knew what to do. He got up from his mattress, brushed off anything that might be crawling on him, and walked out onto Walton Avenue where he extorted ten cents from the first person he saw, an elderly black man on his way home from the night watchman's job he had held for thirty-seven years.

He used the dime to phone a number in Harlem.

"De Lawd be with you," the phone was answered.

"Yeah, yeah," said the Leader for Life. "Ah jes finds out where dey staying."

"Oh?" said the Reverend Josiah Wadson. "Where's that?"

"De Hotel Plaza down in de city."

"Very good," said Wadson. "You knows what to do?"

"Ah knows."

"Good. Take only yo' best mens."

"All my mens be my best mens. 'Ceppin Big-Big Pickens and he still in Nooick."

"Don't mess things up," Wadson said.

"Ah doan."

The Leader for Life of the Saxon Lords hung up the pay telephone in the little candy store. Then because he was Leader for Life and leaders had to display their power, he yanked the receiver cord from the body of the telephone.

He chuckled as he left the store on his way to round up a few of his very, very best men.

137

Chapter Ten

"Where we goin'?" asked Tyrone.

"Back to the hotel."

"Sheeit. Whyn't yo' jes' leave me go?"

"I'm making up my mind whether to kill you or not."

"Dass not right. Ah never did nuffin' you."

"Tyrone, your presence on this earth is doing something to me. You offend me. Now shut up, I'm trying to think."

"Sheeit, dat silly."

"What is?"

"Try'n to think. Nobody try to think. Yo' jes' does it. It be natural."

"Close your face before I close it for you," Remo said.

Tyrone did and slumped in the far corner of the cab's left rear seat.

And as the cab driver tooled down toward Manhattan, four young black men walked along the hallway of the sixteenth floor of the Hotel Plaza toward the suite

here a blood brother bellboy had told them a white
 an was staying with an old Oriental.

Tyrone stayed quiet for a full minute, then could stay
 uiet no more. "Ah doan lahk staying in dat place," he
 id.

"Why not?"

"Dat bed, it be hard."

"What bed?"

"Dat big bed wiffout de mattress. It be hard and hurt
 y back and everyfing."

"The bed?" Remo asked.

"Yeah. Sheeit."

"The big hard white bed?"

"Yeah."

"The big hard white bed that curves up at both
 ids?" Remo asked.

"Yeah. Dat bed."

"That's a bathtub, plungermouth. Close your face."

And while Remo and Tyrone discussed the latest in
 athroom furniture, the Leader for Life of the Saxon
 ords put his hand on the doorknob of Suite 1621 in
 ie Plaza, turned it slightly, and when he found the
 oor unlocked and open, presented a pearly smile of tri-
 mph to his three associates who grinned back and
 randished their brass knuckles and lead-filled saps.

The cab came across the bumpy, rutted Willis Ave-
 ue bridge into northern Manhattan, and as the cab
 ounced up and down on the pitted road surface, Remo
 ondered if anything worked anymore in America.

The road he was riding on felt as if it hadn't been
 aved since it was built. The bridge looked as if it had
 ever been painted. There was a school system that
 idn't teach and a police force that didn't enforce the
 w.

He looked out at the buildings, the geometric row
 ter row of city slum buildings, factories, walkups.

Everything was going to rack and ruin. It sounded li
a law firm that America had on a giant retainer. Ra
and Ruin.

Nothing worked anymore in America.

Meanwhile, the Leader for Life opened the door
Suite 1621 wide. Sitting on the floor in front of the
scribbling furiously on parchment with a quill pen, w
an aged Oriental. Tiny tufts of hair dotted his head.
trace of wispy beard blossomed below his chin. Se
from behind, his neck was thin and scrawny, ready f
wringing. His wrists, jutting out of his yellow robe, we
delicately thin, like the wrists of a skinny old lady. I
must have used a stick the other night in the schoolya
when he hit one of the Lords, the new Leader for L
thought. But they were all little kids anyway. Now
was going to see the real Saxon Lords.

"Come in and close the door," Chiun said witho
turning. "You are welcome to his place." His voice w
soft and friendly.

The Leader for Life motioned his three followers
move into the room, then closed the door and rolled I
eyes toward the old man with a smile. This was gon
be easy. Dat chinky mufu was gonna be a piece of ca
A twinkie even.

Inside the cab as it turned south along the Frank
D. Roosevelt East Side drive, Tyrone's mouth began
work as he tried to formulate a sentence. But Remo w
close to something. There was a thought gnawing at h
and he didn't want it interrupted by Tyrone so
clapped a hand out across Tyrone's mouth and held
there.

It had only been a few years before that a libe
mayor the city's press had loved had left office and so
after one of the city's major elevated highways h
fallen down. Even though millions had been spent

legedly keeping the road repaired, nobody was indicted, no one went to jail, no one seemed to care.

A little bit later it turned out that the same administration had been underestimating the cost of the city's pension agreements by using actuarial tables from the early twentieth century when people's average lifespan was a full twelve years shorter. Nobody cared.

In any other city, there would have been grand jury probes, governor's investigations, mayor's task forces looking into the problem. New York City just yawned and went about its business, its politicians even trying to promote the same mayor, the most inept in a long tradition of inept mayors, into the presidency of the United States.

Who could get upset in New York about just a few more indignities? There were so many indignities day after day.

Remo wondered why, and then a thought came to him.

Was it really America that was so bad? That was falling apart? Out there, across a land of three thousand miles, there were politicians and government officials who tried to do a good job. There were cops more interested in catching muggers than in running classes to teach people to be mugged successfully. There were roads that were paved regularly so that people could drive on them with a good chance of getting to their destination at the same time as their auto's transmission. There were teachers who tried to teach. And often succeeded.

It wasn't America that had failed. That had fallen apart. It was New York, a city of permanently lowered expectations where people lived and surrendered to a lifestyle worse than almost anywhere else in the country. Where people gave up their right to shop in supermarkets at low prices and instead supported neighborhood delicatessens whose prices made the OPEC oil nations look charitable. Where people calmly accepted the fact that it would take forty-five minutes to move five blocks crosstown. Where people surrendered the right to own automobiles because there was no place to park them and no roads fit to drive them on and the streets were unsafe even for automobiles. Where people thought it was a good thing to have block patrols to fight crime, never considering that in most cities, police forces fought crime.

And New Yorkers put up with all of it and smiled to each other at cocktail parties, their shoes still reeking of the scent of dog-doo that covered the entire city to an average depth of seven inches, and clicked their glasses of white wine and said how they just simply wouldn't live anyplace else.

When New York City went bankrupt every eighteen months in one of its regularly scheduled bursts of Faroukian excess, its politicians liked to lecture the country, while begging for handouts, that New York was the heart and soul of America.

But it wasn't, Remo thought. It was the mouth of America, a mouth that never was still, flapping from television stations and networks and radio chains and magazines and newspapers, until even some people living in the Midwest began to believe that if New York City was so bad, well, then, by God, so was the rest of the country.

But it wasn't, Remo realized. America worked. It was New York City that didn't work. And the two of them weren't the same.

It made him feel better about his job.

"You can talk now," Remo said, releasing Tyrone's mouth.

"Ah forgot what ah was gonna say."

"Hold that thought," Remo said.

And as the cab pulled off the FDR drive at Thirty-fourth Street to head west and north again to the Plaza Hotel—its driver figuring to clip his passengers for an extra seventy cents by prolonging the trip—the Leader for Life of the Saxon Lords put his heavy hand on the shoulder of the aged Oriental in Suite 1621 at the Plaza.

"Awright, chinkey Charley," he said. "Yo' comin' wif us. Yo' and that honkey mufu you runs 'round wif." He shook the seated man's shoulder for emphasis. Or tried to shake the shoulder. It seemed to him a little odd that the frail, less than one-hundred-pound body did not move when he tried to shake it.

The old Oriental looked up at the Leader for Life, then at the hand on his left shoulder, then up again and smiled.

"You may leave this world happy," he said with a gracious look. "You have touched the person of the Master of Sinanju."

The Leader for Life giggled. The old gook, he talk funny. Like one of dem faggy honkey perfessers that was always on de television, talking, talking, all de time talking.

He giggled again. Showing de old chink a ting or two was gonna be fun. Real fun.

He took the heavy lead sap out of his back pants pocket, just as a cab pulled up in front of the Plaza on Sixtieth Street sixteen floors below.

Remo paid the driver and steered Tyrone Walker up the broad stone staircase into the lobby of the grand hotel.

Chapter Eleven

There were always sounds in a hotel corridor. There were people with the television on and other people singing as they dressed. Showers ran and toilets flushed and air conditioning hummed. In the Plaza, everything was fudged over with the traffic noise of New York City. The secret in sorting out the different noises was to focus the ears as most people focused their eyes.

When Remo and Tyrone came off the elevator on the sixteenth floor, Remo immediately heard the voices in Suite 1621. He could hear Chiun's voice, and he could hear other voices. Three, perhaps four.

Remo pushed Tyrone into the room first. Chiun was standing near a window, his back toward the street. The afternoon sun silhouetted him dark against the bright light pouring through the thin drapes that ran almost all the way up to the fourteen-foot-high ceiling.

Sitting on the floor facing Chiun were three young

men wearing the blue denim jackets of the Saxon Lords. Their hands were neatly in their laps.

Stuffed off in a corner of the room was another young black man and Remo could tell from the awkward splay of his limbs that it was too late for him to worry about holding his hands properly. Sprinkled haphazardly about his body was a collection of blackjacks and brass knuckles.

Chiun nodded to Remo silently and kept speaking.

"Now try this," he said. "I will obey the law."

The three black youths spoke in unison. "Ah will obeys de law."

"No, no, no," Chiun said. "With me. I, not Ah."

"I," the three men said slowly, with difficulty.

"Very good," Chiun said. "Now. I will obey. Not obeys. Obey."

"I will obey."

"That's correct. Now. The law. Not de law. The. Your tongue must protrude slightly from your mouth and be touched by your upper teeth. Like this." He demonstrated. "The. The. The law."

"The law," the men said slowly.

"Fine. And now the whole thing. I will obey the law."

"Ah will obeys de law."

"What?" shrieked Chiun.

Remo laughed. "By George, I think they've got it. Now try them on the rain in Spain."

"Silence . . . honkey," Chiun spat. He fixed the three youths with hazel eyes that seemed cut from stone. "You. This time, right."

"I. Will. Obey. The. Law." The three men spoke slowly, carefully.

"Again."

"I will obey the law." Faster this time.

"Very good," Chiun said.

"Can we go now, massa?"

"It is not massa. It is Master. Master of Sinanju."

Tyrone said, "Brothers," and the three black men wheeled and stared at him. Their eyes were alive with terror and not even seeing Tyrone standing next to Remo alleviated it.

"Repeat your lessons for the nice gentleman," Chiun said.

As if they were all on one string, the three heads jerked around to face Chiun.

"I will respect the elderly. I will not steal or kill. I will obey the law."

"Very good," Chiun said.

Remo jerked his thumb toward the body in the corner. "Slow learner?"

"I did not have a chance to find out. To teach them, first it was necessary to get their attention. He happened to be the best way to do it, since he had touched my person."

Chiun looked down at the three youths.

"You may stand now."

The three got slowly to their feet. They appeared ill at ease, unsure of what to do with themselves. Tyrone, not having undergone Chiun's good manners school, solved the problem by engaging them in a complicated round robin of hand-slapping greetings, hands apart, hands together, palms up, palms down, palms sliding across other palms. It looked, Remo thought, like pattycake class at a mental institution.

The three young men collected with Tyrone in a corner and whispered to him. Tyrone came back to give the message to Remo as they watched suspiciously.

"De Revin Wadson, he wanna talk to you."

"Who? Oh, yeah. The fence."

"Right. He wanna see you."

"Good. I want to see him too," Remo said.

146

"Dey say he know somefin' about de Missus Mueller," Tyrone said.

"Where do I find him?" Remo asked.

"He gots de big 'partment up in Harlem. Dey takes you dere."

"Good. You can come too."

"Me? Whuffo?"

"In case I need a translator. And you three, get rid of your garbage," Remo said, pointing to the body of the Saxon Lords' Leader for Life, who, since touching Chiun, no longer led. Or lived.

Ingrid did not like the Reverend Josiah Wadson, so at random moments during the day, she jogged the toggle switch on the little black box controlling the strangulation ring. And she smiled when she was rewarded with a roar of pain from wherever in his apartment Wadson was trying to rest.

Before setting foot in Wadson's apartment the night before, she had guessed what she would find. Loud, grotesque, expensive furniture, paid for with money that should have gone to the poor whose case he was always talking up.

But Wadson's life style was lavish, even for her expectations. And unusual.

He had two live-in maids, both young and white, both paid by the federal government as program coordinators for Affirmative Housing II. They looked as if they had majored in Massage Parlor. They dressed like burlesque queens and they were both holding crystal tumblers of whiskey when Ingrid and Wadson returned to the apartment on the fringes of Harlem.

The main living room of the apartment was crammed full, like a junk drawer in a kitchen sink. Statuary, oil paintings, metal sculptures, gold medallions, jewelry were everywhere.

147

"Where did you get all this dross?" she asked Wadson after she dismissed the two maids and told them to take the rest of the week off, a gift for loyal service from grateful government.

"Deys gifts from faithful followers who join me in de Lawd's woik."

"In other words, from poor people you fleeced."

Wadson tried to engage her with a "that's life" grin wide enough to show every one of his thirty-two teeth and most of the gold that lined the biting surfaces.

"I thought as much," she said in disgust. To emphasize the point, she pushed the toggle switch on the black box a millimeter forward. The pain in his groin brought Wadson to his knees.

But she was truly surprised when she saw the rest of the apartment. The living room, kitchen, and two bedrooms were in use. But there were six other rooms in the apartment and each was filled, from floor to ceiling, with television sets, radios, pots and pans, stereo record players, hubcaps. As she went from room to room looking at the treasure trove, it dawned on her what Wadson was. He was a fence for the goods stolen by the street gangs.

It was a suspicion and she asked him if it were true.

Lying was out of the question, he knew. He grinned again.

She left him groaning on the floor of the living room and went into the kitchen to make herself coffee. Only when the coffee had been made and cooled and had consumed, did she return and lighten the pressure of the strangulation ring.

It took an hour of rooting around for Wadson to find the device that had been stolen from the Mueller apartment. He handed it to Ingrid, hoping for some sign of approval.

"You go to bed now," she said.

She stayed in a chair alongside the bed until she was sure Wadson was asleep. Then she telephoned Spesk and described to him the secret device and they shared a laugh.

She spent the night sitting in the chair next to Wadson's bed.

She stood alongside him when he talked to the Saxon Lords about how important it was to find the thin American and the Oriental, and they both learned that the two targets had kidnapped one of the Lords, Tyrone Walker. Wadson was at his unctuous worst in talking to the Lords and it gave her pleasure to toy with the little switch and bring the sweat out on his forehead and cause him to stumble over his own words.

She was still at his side now, as he sat in a chair facing the thin American and the ancient Oriental, and the tall thin black boy who had accompanied them.

"Why he here?" Wadson asked, motioning to Tyrone. "Why is this child here involved in the business of men?" He winced as the pain reminded him of Ingrid standing behind his chair. "And women."

"He's here because I wanted him here," said Remo. "Now what do you want with us?"

"You interested in de Missus Mueller, I hear."

"You hear good," said Remo.

"Well," said Tyrone.

"What?" asked Remo.

"You say he hear good," Tyrone said. "Dat wrong. You sposed say he hear well. Ah learns dat in school."

"Shut up," Remo said. "I'm interested in two things," he said to Wadson. "The person that killed her. And to get some kind of device she may have had."

"Ah gots de dee-vice," said Wadson.

"I wants it," Remo said. "Dammit, Tyrone, now you've got me doing it. I want it."

"Very good," Chiun said to Remo.

149

"I'll get it for you," Wadson said.

He rose slowly to his feet and walked toward a far corner of the room. Chiun caught Remo's eyes and nodded slightly, calling his attention to Wadson's labored walk and obvious pain.

Ingrid watched Wadson with the shrewd suspicious eyes of a chicken farmer looking in the barnyard for fox tracks. Remo watched Ingrid. He guessed her as the source of Wadson's pain but he could not tell what kind. The black minister walked heavily, planting one foot in front of the other delicately, as if he suspected the floor was land-mined.

Wadson opened the drop front of an antique desk and took from inside it a cardboard box almost a foot square. From the box, he lifted a device that looked like a metronome with four arms. Three wires led out of the machine.

He brought it back and handed it to Remo. Wadson walked back to his chair. Ingrid smiled as he raised his eyes to hers in an unspoken appeal to be allowed to sit. She nodded slightly and, shielded from the view of the others by the backs of the large chair, lightened the pressure on the toggle switch slightly. Wadson's sigh of relief filled the room.

"What's it do?" Remo asked, after turning the metronome over and over in his hand. He had never understood machinery. This looked like just another dippy toy.

"Dunno," Wadson said. "But that's it."

Remo shrugged. "One last thing. Big-Big somebody. He killed Mrs. Mueller. Where is he?"

"I hear he's in Newark."

"Where?" asked Remo.

"Ah'm lookin' for him," Wadson said.

"If he's in Newark, how'd you get this?" asked Remo.

"Somebody left it outside my door with a note dat the government was looking for it," Wadson said.

"I think that's crap, but we'll let it pass," Remo said. "I want this Big-Big."

"What'll you do for me?" Wadson said. "Iffen I find him?"

"Let you live," Remo said. "I don't know what's wrong with you, Reverend, but you look like you're in pain. Whatever it is, it'll be nothing compared to what I've got for you, if you're not straight with me."

Wadson raised his hands in a gesture that might have been protest, or the instinctive movement of a man trying to hold back a brick wall that was ready to fall on him.

"I'm not jivin' you," he said. "I got peoples all over de street. I find out soon."

"You let me know right away."

"Who are you anyway?" asked Wadson.

"Let's just say I'm not a private citizen."

"You got family? Mrs. Mueller you family?"

"No," said Remo. I'm an orphan. The nuns raised me. Chiun here is my only family."

"Adopted," Chiun said, lest anyone get the idea that he had white blood in him.

"Where'd you learn to do what you do?" Wadson asked.

"Just what is it I do?"

"I heard you kinda cuffed around de Lawds de other night. That kind of do."

"Just a trick," Remo said.

Tyrone was walking about the room, looking at the statues and the small pieces of crystal and jewelry on the shelves.

"Don' you go liftin' none of them," Wadson yelled. "Dey mine."

Tyrone looked miffed that anyone might think him

capable of theft. He stepped away from the shelf and continued walking around the room. He stopped near Ingrid, saw what she was doing, and with the quick practiced hands of a purse snatcher, reached over and snatched the black box from her hand.

"Look at this," he said, holding it forward to Remo.

"Boy, don' touch that switch," Wadson said. "Please."

"Which switch?" said Tyrone. "Dis one here?" He put his fingers on the toggle switch.

"Please, boy. Let go of it."

"Give it back to me, Tyrone," Ingrid said coolly. "Just hand it back to me."

"What's it do?" Tyrone asked.

"It's a pain-killing device for people with migraine headaches," she said. "The reverend suffers greatly from that feeling of tightness around his head. That relieves it. Please give it back to me." She extended her hand for the little black box.

Tyrone looked at Remo who shrugged. "Give it back to her," he said.

"I do," said Tyrone. He started to extend the little box, but couldn't resist giving the switch a tiny push.

"*Aiieee,*" screamed Wadson.

Ingrid snatched the box from Tyrone's hands and quickly moved the switch back. Wadson sipped air in relief, so deeply it sounded as if someone had turned on a vacuum cleaner. He was still hissing when they left. Ingrid stood behind him smiling.

In the hallway walking downstairs, Remo asked "What do you think, Little Father?"

"About what?"

"About Reverend Wadson?"

"There is less there than meets the eye," said Chiun.

"And about this machine of the Muellers?"

"It is a machine. All machines are alike. They break Send it to Smith. He likes to play with toys."

The device was delivered to Smith's office in Rye, New York at two A.M. by a cabdriver who had been paid with half of a hundred dollar bill and a grinding brief pain in his right kidney. He was told to deliver it fast and he would get the other half of the hundred at the Hotel Plaza desk and would not get the rest of the pain.

It was the middle of the night and Tyrone was asleep in the bathroom when there was a knock on the door.

"Who is it?" Remo called.

"The bellboy, sir. There's a phone call for you. And your phone is out of order."

"I know. I'll take it in the lobby."

"I received the package," Smith told Remo when he picked up the telephone downstairs.

"Oh, Smitty. Nice to hear from you again. You recruit my replacement yet?"

"I only hope that if I do he will be more reasonable to deal with than you are." Remo was surprised. Smith never showed temper. Or any other emotion for that matter. The realization that this was a first chastened Remo.

"What's with the device?" he asked. "Any value?"

"None. It's a lie detector that runs on induction."

"What's that mean?"

"They don't have to attach wires to the subject. So it's useful in questioning a suspect whom you don't want to know he's a suspect. You can ask him questions and hook that device up to the bottom of his chair and it'll register whether he's telling the truth or not."

"Sounds good," Remo said.

"Fair," said Smith. "We've got better stuff now. And with pentothal, nobody in tradework uses devices much anymore."

"Okay, so I'm done here and now I can get about my other business?"

"Which is?"

"Finding the man who killed that old lady to steal a machine that didn't have any value."

"That'll have to wait," Smith said. "You're not done."

"What else?" Remo asked.

"Don't forget. I told you about Colonel Speskaya being in the country and two other weapons he was trying to get his hands on."

"Probably more lie detectors," Remo said.

"I doubt it. He's too good to be fooled. So that's your job. Find out what he's after and get it for us."

"And when I'm done with that?"

"Then you can do anything you want. Really, Remo, I don't know why this is so important to you."

"Because somebody out there put an icepick in an old lady's eye just for fun. Killing for sport cheapens the work I do. I'm going to keep the amateurs out."

"Making the world safe for assassins?" Smith asked.

"Making it unsafe for animals."

"You do it. I just hope you can tell the difference," said Smith before the telephone line clicked in Remo's ear.

Remo put down the telephone with the same faint feeling of unease that conversations with Smith always gave him. It was as if, without saying a word, Smith entered a continuous moral judgment against Remo. But where was the immorality since it had been Smith who virtually kidnaped Remo from his straight middle-America life to make him a killer? Were moral judgments only valid for what other people did, and expediency the only yardstick one used on himself?

Chiun noticed the puzzled look on Remo and was about to speak when they heard the scratching on the bathroom door. Simultaneously, they decided to ignore Tyrone.

"You worry, my son, because you are yet a child."

"Dammit, Chiun, I'm no child. I'm a grown man.

154

And I don't like what's going down. Smith's got me running around looking for two more secret weapons and I just . . . well, I'm just not interested in it all anymore."

"You will always be a child if you expect men to be more than they are. If you are walking through the woods, you do not get angry at a tree that happened to grow up directly in your path. The tree could not help it. It existed. You do not sit on the ground in front of that tree and lecture it. You ignore it. And if you cannot ignore it, you remove it. So you must act with people. They are, for the most part, like trees. They do what they do because they are what they are."

"And so I should ignore all those that I can and remove those that I can't?"

"Now you are seeing the light of wisdom," Chiun said, folding his hands in front of him with a movement as smooth as that of an underwater plant.

"Chiun, the world you give me is a world without morality. Where nothing counts for anything except keeping your elbow straight and breathing right and attacking correctly. You give me no morality and that makes me happy. Smith gives me a shitpot full of morality and it disgusts me. But I like his world better than yours."

Chiun shrugged. "That is because you do not understand the real meaning of my world. I do not give you a world without morality. I give you a world of total morality but the only morality you totally control is your own. Be moral. You can do no greater thing in your life." He moved his arms around in a large slow circle. "Try to make other people moral and you are trying to ignite ice with a match."

Tyrone stopped scratching. "Hey, when ah gets out of here?" his muffled voice called. Remo looked toward the locked bathroom door.

"And him?"

"He is what he is," Chiun said. "A candy wrapper on

155

the street, an orange peel in the garbage. A man who decides to worry about everyone will have no shortage of things to keep him busy."

"You say I should let him go?"

"I say you should do whatever makes you a better person," Chiun said.

"And what about the man who killed Mrs. Mueller? Let him go too?"

"No."

"Why not?"

"Because you need that one if you are to be at peace with yourself. So find him and do what it is you wish with him."

"That's a selfish view of life, Little Father. Tell me. Don't you ever wish you could just get rid of all the evil people in the world, all the garbage, all the animals?"

"No," Chiun said.

"Did you ever?" Remo asked.

Chiun smiled. "Of course. I was a child once too, Remo."

Chapter Twelve

When Remo's cab pulled up in front of Reverend Wadson's apartment building, the crowd was pulsating on the street and sidewalk. Some carried signs, others were chanting. "Brutality. Atrocity."

Remo tapped the driver on the shoulder and motioned him to the curb.

"Wait here for me," he said.

The cabbie looked at the two hundred people milling around across the street, then swiveled on his seat to look at Remo.

"I'm not staying here, buddy. Not with that gang over there. They'll use me for chum if they spot me."

"I'd like to stay and discuss it with you," said Remo, "but I don't have the time." His hand slipped forward past the driver, turned the ignition key off, and plucked it from its slot on the steering column, all in one deft movement. "You wait. Lock the doors, but wait. I'll be right back."

"Where you going?"

"Over there." Remo motioned to the apartment house.

"You'll never be back."

Remo dropped the keys into his trouser pocket. As he trotted across the street, he could hear the heavy mechanical click of the four door locks in the cab behind him.

The crowd was being kept at bay by the locked front doors of the apartment building. Inside the lobby, a uniformed doorman kept motioning the people to leave.

"What's going on?" Remo asked the question of a young man with a shaved head and a Fu Manchu mustache who stood on the fringe of the crowd.

The man looked at Remo. His face curled down in disgust and he turned away silently.

"We'll try one more time," Remo said gently. "What's going on?" He punctuated the question, using his right hand to grip the muscles on both sides of the man's lower spine.

The man straightened up from the pain, taller than he had ever stood before in his life.

"They got Reverend Wadson."

"Who's they?"

"I don't know who they is. His enemies. Enemies of the people. The oppressors."

"What do you mean, they got Wadson?"

"He's dead. They killed him. Cut him up and butchered him. Let go, that hurts."

Remo did not let go. "And 'they' did it?"

"That's right."

"And what do these people want? Why are they marching around here?"

"They want justice."

"They think you get it by singing?"

The young man tried to shrug. It felt as if his shoulders were going up and leaving his spinal column behind. He changed his mind.

"Police arrive yet?" asked Remo.

"They just been called."

"Thank you. A pleasure talking with you," Remo said.

He released the young man and moved along the perimeter of the crowd. If he went through the front door, he'd just open a path for this mob. Behind him, the young man tried to marshal his breath to sic the crowd on Remo but every time he tried to fill his lungs to shout, the pain returned to his back. He decided that silence was golden.

Remo surged forward and back with the crowd, moving from spot to spot, being seen, then disappearing, visible, invisible, never in anyone's field of vision for more than a split second, until he had moved to the alley alongside the apartment building. The alley was barred by a locked iron gate eight feet high, with spikes atop it, and barbed wire laced in and out of the spikes.

Remo grabbed the heavy lock and wrenched it with his right hand and the gate gave way smoothly. Remo slipped aside, then punished the lock again until it merged with the metal of the fence and stayed closed. The fire escapes were in the rear of the building and Remo went up the fourteen stories until he got to a window outside Wadson's apartment. He was ready to push open the window when the drapes inside were flung back and the window was opened.

Ingrid stifled a scream when she saw Remo on the fire escape, then said, "Thank God you're here."

"What happened?" Remo asked.

"Josiah's dead." Tears poured from her eyes.

"I know. Who did it?"

"A blond man. With a foreign accent. I was sleeping but he came into the apartment and I heard him talking to Josiah and then I heard screams and when I got up, Josiah was all cut up and dead. The blond man was running out the door. I called the doorman to stop him, but I guess he escaped."

"Why are you running away before the police arrive?"

"This'll cost me my job if I'm found here. I was supposed to be doing a film documentary. I wasn't supposed to fall in love with a black man." She climbed out onto the fire escape. "I loved that man. I really did." She buried her face in Remo's shoulder and wept. "Please get me away from here."

"All right," Remo said.

Remo closed the window again, then hustled her down the fire escape and out another alley behind the building. It exited onto another side street, secured by an identical heavy iron gate. Remo snapped the steel with his hands. He turned to see Ingrid staring at the twisted metal.

"How'd you do that?" she asked.

"Must have been defective," Remo answered, as he steered her around the corner to the cab. The driver was lying on the front seat of the cab, trying to keep out of sight and Remo had to thump loudly on the window to get him to look up. Remo gave him his keys back and the driver peeled rubber leaving the neighborhood. The crowd had already grown larger in front of the apartment building because the word had spread that the television cameramen were coming and no one wanted to miss his chance to be on the tube. Especially the veterans of the civil rights riots who left their liquor stores and their card games to come over and carry signs.

When Ingrid came into the Plaza suite with Remo, Chiun said nothing, but saw the boxy lump hidden inside her purse.

While she was in the bathroom, Remo said,

160

"Wadson's dead. I got her out of there. She's staying with us awhile."

"Good ting," Tyrone said. "She can sleep in my bed. She some hunk of honkey."

"Lacks bulk," Chiun said.

"Hands off," Remo said to Tyrone.

"Sheeit," said Tyrone and went back to watching the rerun of *Leave it to Beaver*. Chiun changed it to *Sesame Street*.

While Remo had been at Wadson's apartment, the management had installed a new telephone in the suite. And now, while Ingrid was at the drugstore in the Plaza lobby, the phone rang.

"Yeah," said Remo, expecting to hear Smith's voice.

"This is Speskaya," a voice said. There was something in the voice that Remo remembered. But where? Who? The voice was not accented but sounded as if it should have been. "I killed Wadson."

"What do you want?" Remo asked.

"To offer you work. You and the Oriental gentleman."

"Sure. Let's talk about it," Remo said.

"That is just too easily said for me to believe you."

"Would you believe I want your job if I say I don't want it?" Remo asked.

"Job?" Chiun said. He was sitting on the sofa. He looked toward Remo. "Someone is offering us a job?"

Remo raised his hand to silence Chiun.

Speskaya said, "It is difficult to gauge your motives." The voice was familiar, but Remo could not put it together with a face.

"I can't help that," Remo said.

"What is the offer?" Chiun said.

Remo waved a hand to shush him.

"You work for a country which is breaking down,"

161

Speskaya said. "People are butchered in their homes. You, who are no stranger to death, find that offensive. Why not come over with us?"

"Look, let's stop mousing around. I've got a secret weapon you want. I'll give it to you. You tell me about the secret weapons you're working on and we'll be square and you can go back to Russia," Remo said.

"Secret weapons? I'm working on?"

"Yeah. Two of them."

There was a long pause, then a boyish laugh over the telephone. "Of course. Two secret weapons."

"What's so funny?" Remo said.

"Never mind," Speskaya said.

"Is it a deal?"

"No. The device you have is nothing but a low-level biofeedback device that works off induction and is virtually without worth."

"And your two secret weapons?" Remo said.

"They are of great worth. Great worth."

"I bet," said Remo.

"There is a club called The Iron Dukes on Walton Avenue. I will meet you there tonight. I will tell you about my weapons and I will expect your answer about working for us. Nine o'clock."

"I'll be there."

"The Oriental too."

"We'll be there," Remo said.

"Good thing, fella. Look forward to seeing you," Speskaya said. And as the telephone clicked, Remo recognized the voice. It was that jovial "fella" that did it. The man he had met at the excavation at the Mueller's apartment, the man whose knee he had banged up. Tony Spesk, alias Speskaya, Russian colonel and spy.

"Tonight," Remo said to Chiun, just as Ingrid came back into the room. "We'll find out what two weapons he's working on."

162

"And then?"

"Then we get rid of him and that's that," Remo said.

"You have no idea what his special weapons are?" Chiun asked.

Remo shrugged. "Who cares? More machinery."

"You are a fool," said Chiun.

A few moments later, Ingrid remembered something she had forgotten at the drugstore. She went back downstairs and called a number on a pay phone.

"Anthony," she said. "I just overheard. They plan to kill you tonight."

"Too bad," Spesk said. "They would have been most valuable additions to our arsenal."

"What now?" Ingrid asked.

"Use the white ring. And let me know how it works."

On Halsey Street in Newark, the burly black man found what he was looking for. He had passed up two Volkswagens to find an unlocked car big enough for him to sit in comfortably.

He opened the door of the new Buick and hunched over close to the dashboard, bridging the ignition with a pair of alligator clips he carried in his pocket. From his belt, he unhooked a huge ring of keys, dwarfed by his big heavy hand, and sorted through them until he found one that seemed right and put it in the ignition. He turned it, the starter growled, and the motor started smoothly.

Big-Big Pickens drove into traffic with a smile on his face. He was going home and getting those Saxon Lords straightened out.

Just turns his back, and some honkey and little old chink, they been busting up the gang, and two of the leaders dead, and the Reverend Wadson dead, and about time for all this nonsensery to end. He patted the ice pick he carried in his hip pocket, its business end stuck into a cork. On a whim he removed it and slammed it deep into the car seat.

And he smiled again.

Chapter Thirteen

In the living room Remo had changed into a black tee shirt and black slacks.

"Remo." Ingrid's voice was a soft call from the bedroom door.

Remo nodded and stood. Chiun was wearing a thin black robe. Tyrone still wore the same denim jacket, jeans, and dirty white tee shirt he had worn for three days.

"We'll be leaving right away," Remo said, looking through the window at nighttime New York. "But there's something to do first."

The old man nodded.

Inside, Ingrid sat on the edge of the bed. She had just come from the shower and wore only a thin blue satin robe.

"Must you go?" she said to Remo. With her faint European accent, her voice sounded wistful and lost.

"Afraid so."

"That man is a bad man. He killed Josiah."

"You mean Spesk? Just another agent. No problem."

She put her hands up to Remo's arms and pulled him closer to her, until his knees touched hers.

"I would be shattered if you were hurt . . . or . . ."

"Killed? I don't expect to be."

"But he is a killer."

"That's right, isn't it? And you saw him running away after he killed Wadson."

Ingrid nodded. She trailed her hands around Remo's back until they were at the base of his spine. She pulled him to her and buried her face in his stomach.

"Yes." Her voice seemed choked. "I saw him. I will never forget him."

"Tall, lean man. Thinning blond hair. Little scar over the left eye."

He felt her head nod against his stomach. Then he felt her hands at his waist, fumbling with the belt of his trousers.

"Remo," she said softly. "this may be strange, but in just these few hours . . . there has come to be . . . I can't explain it. You'll laugh."

"Never laugh at a woman in love," Remo said.

His trousers were open now and she busied her hands and her face with his body.

Then she fell back onto the bed, her right hand holding his left wrist and pulling him down to her.

"Come, Remo. Make love to me. Now. I can't wait."

The front of her robe fell open and Remo slipped down onto her blond goddess body. Mechanically, he began sex. He felt her right arm leave his wrist and reach up under the pillow at the headboard of the bed. She put her left arm around his neck and pulled his face down to her so he could not see what she was doing.

He felt the slight shift in her body weight as her right hand returned toward her waist. He felt the fingers slide

166

in between their stomachs and then he felt the constriction as the hard white metal ring was placed on his body.

Remo pulled back and looked down at the white ring. Ingrid reached again over her head and had the small black box in her hand, with the red toggle switch in the center.

She smiled at him, a vicious smile that was as foreign to love as it was to warmth.

"And now, the charade ends."

"As all good charades must," Remo said.

"Do you know what that ring is?"

"Some kind of pressure device, I guess," Remo said.

"As effective as a guillotine." She scootched herself up into a sitting position in bed.

"Is this what you used on Wadson?" Remo asked.

"Yes. I used it all over his body. To mutilate him. He was gross. You learn very quickly."

"No," said Remo. "I didn't learn. I knew."

It was time for Ingrid to be surprised. "You knew?"

"When you said you saw Spesk running away after killing Wadson. I broke Spesk's kneecap three nights ago. He isn't doing much running these days."

"And yet you came in here? Like a lamb to slaughter?"

"I'm not exactly a lamb."

"You will be. A lamb. Or a gelding."

"What is it you want?" Remo asked.

"It is simple. You join Spesk and me. You work with us."

"I don't think so," Remo said.

"The old one would. I have heard him today. He would go wherever the money is best. Why is he so reasonable and you so unreasonable?"

"We're both unreasonable. Just in different ways," Remo said.

"Then your answer is no."

"You got it, sweetheart."

She looked down at the red switch in her hand.

"You know what happens next, don't you?"

"Go ahead," Remo said. "But know this. You die. You can play with your toy there and maybe hurt me but I'll have time to kill you and you know I will. And you will die very slowly. Very painfully."

His deep brown eyes that seemed to have no pupils met hers. They stared at each other. She looked away, and as if backing down from his stare had thrown her into a rage, she slammed her hand onto the red toggle switch, pushing it all the way forward. Baring her teeth and gums with lips twisted open in hatred, she looked up at Remo.

He still knelt in the same place on the bed. His face showed no emotion, no pain. Her eyes met his again and Remo laughed. He reached onto the bed and picked up the two halves of the white ring, split cleanly, like an undersized doughnut cut in two by a very precise knife. He tossed them to her.

"Called muscle control, kid."

He stood up and zipped his trousers and fastened his belt. Ingrid scurried across the bed and reached into her handbag on the end table. She pulled out a small pistol and rolled toward Remo, aiming the gun at him in an easy, unhurried motion.

As her finger began to tighten on the trigger, Remo picked up half of the white ring and tossed it at her, skidding it off the ends of his fingertips with enough force that it whirred as it traveled the four feet to Ingrid.

Her finger squeezed the trigger just as the piece of the ring hit the barrel of the gun with hammer force, driving the muzzle upward under Ingrid's chin. It was too late for her brain to recall the firing signal.

The gun exploded, one muffled shot, which ripped upward through Ingrid's chin, passed through the bottom half of her skull, and buried itself in her brain.

Eyes still open, lips still pulled back in a cat snarl of anger, she dropped the gun and fell onto her side on the bed. The gun clanked to the floor. A thin trail of blood poured from the bullet wound in her chin, slipping down throat and shoulders until it reached the blue satin of her robe which absorbed it and turned almost black.

Remo looked at the dead body, shrugged casually, and left the room.

In the living room, without turning from the window through which he assayed New York City, Chiun said, "I'm glad that's over with."

"Did ah hears a shot?" asked Tyrone.

"You sure do," said Remo. "Time to go."

"Go where?"

"You're going home, Tyrone."

"You lettin' me go?"

"Yeah."

"Good thing," said Tyrone, jumping to his feet. "So long."

"Not so quick. You're going with us," Remo said.

"Whuffo?"

"Just in case this big bear or whatever his name is is round. I want you to point him out to me."

"He a big mean muvver. He kill me if he find out I finger him for you."

"And what will I do?" Remo asked.

"Aw, sheeeit," said Tyrone.

Chapter Fourteen

All the streetlights were out on the block which house
the Iron Dukes' clubrooms.

Remo stood under one of the unworking lights a
touched his toe to the broken glass on the street. T
block seemed weighted down with summer dampness. A
the building lights on the street were out too and Tyro
looked around nervously.

"Ah don' like dis place," he said. "Too dark."

"Somebody made it that way for us," Remo said. "A
they there, Chiun?"

"How many of them?"

"Yes," Chiun said. "Across the street."

"Many bodies," Chiun said. "Perhaps thirty."

"Wha' you talkin' 'bout?" Tyrone asked.

"Tyrone," Remo explained patiently. "Somebody j
busted all the streetlights to make this block dark. A
now whoever did it is hiding around here, waiting

don't look around like that, you dip . . . hiding around here waiting for us."

"Ah don' like dat," Tyrone said. "What's we gone do?"

"What we're going to do is Chiun and I are going up to see Spesk. You're going to stay down here and see if you see Big-Big whatsisface. And when I come down, you point him out to me."

"Ah don' wanna."

"You better," Remo said. They left Tyrone standing at the curb and followed a small single light upstairs into a large office that had a desk at the far end of the room.

Behind the desk sat Tony Spesk, good old Tony, appliance salesman, Carbondale, Illinois, AKA Colonel Speskaya, NKVD. His gooseneck lamp was twisted so it shone in his visitors' faces.

"We meet again," Spesk said. "Ingrid is dead, of course."

"Of course," Remo said. He took a few steps forward into the room.

"Before you try anything foolish," Spesk said, "I should advise you that there is an electronic eye in this room. If you attempt to reach me, you will break the beam and set off a crossfire of machine guns. Do not be foolish."

Chiun looked at the walls of the vacant room and nodded. On the left wall, there were electric eye units starting six inches above the floor, and then one each foot higher until they stopped eight feet above the floor, one foot below the ceiling. He nodded to Remo.

"Now, have you considered my offer?" Spesk said.

"Yes. Considered and rejected," Remo said.

"That's a shame," said Spesk. "I would not have thought you were patriots."

"Patriotism has nothing to do with it," said Remo. "We just don't like you people."

"Russians have been worthless since the time of Ivan the Great," said Chiun.

"The Terrible, you mean," Spesk said.

"The Great," Chiun insisted.

"He paid on time," Remo explained.

"Well, then I guess there's nothing more to talk about," Spesk said.

"One thing," said Remo. "These two weapons you're after. What are they?"

"You don't know, do you?" asked Spesk after a pause.

"No," said Remo.

"The old man knows though. Don't you?"

Remo looked over to see Chiun nod.

"Well, if you know so much, Chiun, why didn't you tell me?" Remo asked.

"Sometimes it is easier to talk to Tyrone," Chiun said.

"Tell me now. What two weapons?" Remo said.

"You," said Chiun. "And me."

"Us?" Remo said.

"We," Chiun said.

"Sheeit. All this for that."

"Enough," said Spesk. "We cannot deal and that is that. You may leave and later I will leave. And perhaps we will meet again someday."

"We're the weapons you wanted?" Remo asked again.

Spesk nodded, his thin blond hair splashing about his face as he did.

"You're a jerk," Remo said.

"Time now for you to leave," Spesk said.

"Not yet," Remo said. "You understand it's nothing personal but, well, Chiun and I don't like too many people to know about what work we do and who we work for. And you know a little too much."

"Remember the electric eyes," Spesk said confidently.

172

"Remember the Alamo," said Remo. He rocked back
to his left foot, then moved forward toward the invisible strings of light reaching from left wall to right wall.
Three feet before reaching the beams, he turned toward
the wall, reached up high with his right foot, followed
with his left foot and launched his body upward. His
stomach came within an eighth of an inch of hitting the
ceiling as he turned onto his back, floating over the
topmost beam as if it were the bamboo pole at a high-
jump event. Then Remo was over the lights, onto
desk's side of the room. He landed on his feet sound-
lessly.

The Russian colonel's eyes opened wide in shock and
horror. He got heavily to his feet behind the desk, his
left knee still defective where Remo had damaged it.

He moved away from Remo.

"Listen," he said. His Chicago middle-America accent
had vanished. He spoke now with the thick guttural
lisp of a native Russian. "You don't want to kill me.
I'm the only one who can get you out of here alive. It's a
trap."

"We know that," Remo said. "We'll take our
chances."

He moved toward Spesk and Spesk dove for the desk
drawer. His hand was into the drawer closing around a
gun, when Remo snatched up the gooseneck lamp from
the desk and looped it over Spesk's head, around his
throat, and yanked him back from the revolver. He tied
the gooseneck in one large knot and dropped Spesk's
body to the floor. So much for the Russian spies; so
much for the secret weapons.

As Remo was vaulting back over the electric eyes, now
visible in the pitch-black room, he said, "Why didn't you
tell me, Chiun? About the weapons?"

"Who can explain anything to a white man?" Chiun

173

said. He was already at the door and going down t
steps.

Except for the sucking of air by people who did
know how to breathe correctly, the street outside t
Iron Dukes' was silent when Remo and Chiun ca
through the door and stood on the sidewalk.

"Still say thirty?" Remo asked.

Chiun cocked his head to listen. "Thirty-four,"
said.

"That's not bad. I hope one of them is the one
want. Where the hell is Tyrone?" Remo said.

"One of the thirty-four," Chiun said, just as th
heard a roar. Tyrone's roar.

"There they are. Get dem. Get dem. Dey kidnap
and everyfing."

Like predatory animals whose coats blended in wi
the grass, the black youths of the Saxon Lords rose
out of their protective coloration of night and with
full-throated roar charged across the street toward Re
and Chiun.

"When I get that Tyrone," Remo said, "I'm going
fix him good."

"Back on that, are you?" Chiun said, just as the fi
wave of attackers reached them, brandishing clubs a
chains, knives and tire irons.

Chiun blended a four-armed lug wrench into t
thoracic cavity of one bruiser and drifted to the left, l
black robe swirling about him, as Remo went towa
the right.

"Damned right," Remo called. "He needs a go
lesson. Where are you, Tyrone?"

The air was filled with rocks being thrown by t
Saxon Lords, hitting only other Saxon Lords. O
thought he saw Remo drifting by him and slashed o

wildly with his seven-inch bladed hunting knife, neatly severing the carotid artery of his cousin.

"Where the hell is he?" Remo's voice rang out. "Now I know how Stanley felt looking for Livingstone."

Remo ducked under one flailing tire iron and came up with the tips of his fingers into a throat.

He went around two more of the gang who had started to fight with each other because one had stepped on the other's new platforms and scuffed the leather.

"Tell me if you see Tyrone," Remo said.

"Tyrone, he back dere," said one of the young men, just before his head was laid open by a chain swung by his comrade-in-arms.

"Thank you," Remo said. To the other he said, "Good form."

He was in the heart of the gang now, moving away from the Iron Dukes' building, working slowly across the street.

And on the sidewalk across the street, Big-Big Pickens saw the Saxon Lords disorganized and dropping. He craned his neck to look over the crowd but could see no sign of the white man or the old Oriental. But every few seconds, two more Saxon Lords would drop and he could tell where they had been.

He decided that Newark was really nice this time of year and stuck his icepick back into the protective cork and put it into his rear pocket, then turned and walked away.

"There you are, Tyrone," Remo said. Tyrone was standing alone at the fringe of the crowd. "You've got one helluva nerve."

Tyrone put his hands up to protect himself, just as Chiun arrived.

"Here I thought we were friends and all," Remo said.

"We is. I just findin' Big-Big for you. Dere he goes."

Tyrone pointed to a huge black figure running down the street.

"Thanks, Tyrone. Chiun, you keep an eye on him."

Remo was off then, running after Big-Big Pickens.

The big man heard the roar of the street fight behind him and glanced over his shoulder. He felt a tingle of fear in his shoulders as he saw the thin white man, wearing the black slacks and tee shirt, running after him, gaining on him. Then he stopped.

He nothing but some skinny honkey, he thought. He ducked into an alley, moving back into the shadows, waiting for Remo to enter. He took his pick from his pocket and held it over his head, ready to bring it down into the base of Remo's skull when he entered the alley.

He heard Remo's footsteps approaching on the run. Big-Big coughed, with a smile on his face, just to let the white man know where he was. In case he hadn't seen Pickens enter the alley.

The running stopped. And then there was no sound.

Pickens pressed his back against the brick wall of the building, waiting for Remo to be silhouetted in the dim light at the alley's entrance. But he saw nothing.

He waited a few long seconds that seemed like minutes, and then took a step away from the wall. Remo must be lurking outside the alley waiting for him to come out. Well, they would see who would outwait the other, he thought.

Big-Big Pickens felt a small touch on his shoulder. He wondered what it was. It turned into a tap.

Pickens wheeled around. Remo was standing there, a broad smile on his face.

"Looking for me?" he asked.

Big-Big recoiled in shock, then slashed down with the icepick he remembered holding over his head. Remo moved back slightly, seemingly no more than an inch or two, but the pick missed.

"You're Pickens?" Remo said.

"Yeah, mufu."

"You're the one who did in the old lady? Mrs. Mueller?"

"Yeah. Ah did it."

"Tell me. Was it fun? Did you enjoy it?"

"Nots much fun as giving you dis," said Pickens, running forward like a bull, the pick held close to his stomach, waiting to close on Remo so he could bring one heavy hand up and bury the point deep into Remo's belly.

He looked up and stopped. He could not see the white man. Where was he? He turned. The man was behind him.

"You're really garbage, you know that?" Remo said.

"Ah garbages yo", said Big-Big, charging again.

Remo moved out of his way and tripped the huge man. Pickens sprawled across the alley. The rough concrete surface scratched his cheek.

"You know," Remo said, standing over Pickens. "I don't think I really like you. On your feet."

Big-Big got to his knees and put a hand down to steady himself and lift himself to his feet.

Then he felt a foot smash into his broad nose. He could hear the bones crack and a whoosh of blood come pouring down through his nostrils.

His head snapped backward but he recovered and got to his feet.

"You're the big pick man on the block, huh?" Remo said. "Is your pick as sharp as this?"

And Pickens felt what seemed to be a knifeblade in the left side of his stomach. He looked down for the blood, but he saw nothing. Only the white man's hand slowly pulling away. But the pain. The pain. It felt like a hot poker was lying on his skin, and he knew that hurt, because he had done it to someone one night.

"As sharp as that?" Remo taunted.

Holding his icepick, Pickens turned, flailing about with his right arm, trying to find his tormentor.

But Remo was behind him. And Pickens heard the voice again, mocking him. "As hard as this?"

And there was a blow into Pickens's back. He could feel it stowing in his ribs on the right. And then it was repeated on the left side and more ribs went.

"Did the old lady scream when you killed her, Pig-Pig?" Remo asked. "Did she scream like this?"

He tried not to but the pain in his neck demanded nothing but a scream. There were fingers on his neck and they felt as if they were tearing through his skin and flesh to get to his adam's apple. Pickens screamed. And screamed again.

"Do you think it hurt this bad, Pig-Pig? When you killed her?"

He wheeled around, his hands clutching out in front of him, but they grabbed nothing. His arms closed on empty air. He felt himself being propelled backwards and he crashed into the brick wall like an overripe tomato and slithered to the concrete. His icepick fell from his hand and clattered onto the ground.

There was a terrible pain where his right leg used to be. He tried to move it, but the leg no longer responded. And there was more pain as his left leg gave way with a snap. And then his stomach felt as if it were being torn apart by rats; he could feel what seemed like giant pieces of it being torn away, and he screamed, a long, long, lingering scream that celebrated agony and welcomed death.

And then there was a white face right in front of him and it was leaning close to him, and it said, "You killed her with the pick, animal, and now you're going to learn what it was like."

And then there was a ringing black starshine of pain at his left eye where the icepick was stuck. He could not see left anymore. And then the pain stopped and the big black man fell forward, his head smashing onto the concrete of the alley with a dull empty thud. The last thing he'd seen was that the white man had clean fingernails.

Remo spat down at the body and stepped out of the alley, back onto the sidewalk as a car came roaring down the street past him. It was followed by two more cars.

Remo looked down the street where the Saxon Lords were involved in a massive free-for-all, as it was suddenly illuminated by the onrushing headlights. Coming down the block the other way were three more automobiles.

The cars screeched to a stop and men jumped out. Remo could see they were carrying weapons. And then he heard a familiar voice. It was Sergeant Pleskoff.

"All right. Shoot 'em. Shoot the bastards. Shoot 'em right in the whites of their goddam eyes. We'll show 'em. America's had enough of this goddam violence. Kill 'em all. No survivors."

Remo was able to pick Pleskoff out. He was waving his arm over his head in a passable imitation of Errol Flynn's passable imitation of General Custer. He was wearing civilian clothes. So were the other dozen men who began firing into the mob with Police Specials and shotguns.

Then Chiun was at Remo's side, with Tyrone in tow. Tyrone was looking back over his shoulder as the streets began to fill up with fallen bodies.

"Did you want him?" Chiun asked Remo.

"No. Not any more," said Remo.

Tyrone turned toward Remo, his eyes wide with fright.

"Ah doan wan' go back there."

179

"Why not?"

"It gettin' dangerous on de streets aroun' here," Tyrone said. "Can ah hang out wif you?"

Remo shrugged. Down the street the orgy of bulleting was slowing down. The screams were dying away. Few people were left standing. Pleskoff's voice kept roaring: "Shoot 'em all. We'll straighten this town out."

Chiun turned toward the voice also.

"I've created a goddam Wyatt Earp," Remo said.

"It is always the way when a man deals in vengeance," Chiun said. "Always the way."

"Always the way," Remo repeated.

"Allus de way," Tyrone said.

"Shut up," Remo said.

"Shut up," Chiun said.

Back at the Plaza, Chiun fished into one of his large lacquered trunks for a scroll of parchment and a bottle of ink and a large quill pen.

"What are you doing?" Remo asked.

"Writing for the history of Sinanju," Chiun said.

"About what?"

"About how the Master brought wisdom to his disciple by teaching him that vengeance is destructive."

"Be sure to write that it feels good too," Remo said.

He watched as Tyrone peered over Chiun's shoulder and then, behind Chiun's back, looked into the open trunk.

Chiun began writing. "You must see, Remo, that it would have done nothing to act vengefully against Tyrone. He is not responsible. There is nothing he can do about what he is."

Tyrone at that moment was slipping out the front door of the apartment.

"I'm glad you feel that way, Chiun," Remo said.

180

"Ummmm," the old man said, writing. "Why?"

"Because Tyrone just beat it with one of your diamond rings."

The quill pen flew upwards and stuck in the plaster ceiling. The bottle of ink flew off in another direction. Chiun dropped the the parchment scroll and moved quickly to his feet to the trunk. He bent forward, burying his head inside it, then stood up. His face was pale as he turned to Remo.

"He did. He did."

"He went thataway," Remo said, pointing to the door. But before he finished the sentence, Chiun was already out into the hall.

It was 11:30 P.M. Time to call Smith at the special 800 area code number that was open only twice a day.

"Hello," said Smith's acid-soaked voice.

"Hi, Smitty. How's it going?"

"I presume you have a report to make," Smith said.

"Just a minute." Remo covered the mouthpiece of the telephone. Outside the door, down the hallway near the elevator, he could hear thumping. And groans. And somebody weeping. Remo nodded.

"Yeah," Remo said. "Well, Spesk is dead. The guy who killed Mrs. Mueller is dead. There are at least a dozen New York City cops who are beginning to do something about criminals. All in all, I'd say a fair day's work."

"What about . . ."

"Just a minute," Remo said as the door to the suite opened. In walked Chiun, polishing his diamond ring on the black sleeve of his kimono, blowing on it, then polishing.

"You got it back," Remo said.

"Obviously."

"No vengeance, I hope," Remo said.

Chiun shook his head. "I suited the punishment to

181

the crime. He stole my diamond; I stole his ability to steal again for a long time."

"What'd you do?"

"I reduced his finger bones to putty. And warned him that if I ever saw him again, I would not treat him so kindly."

"I'm glad you weren't vengeful, Little Father. Be sure to put that in your history."

Chiun scooped up the parchment scroll and dumped it into the lacquered chest. "I don't feel like writing any more tonight."

"There's always tomorrow." Remo turned his attention back to the telephone. "You were saying, Smitty?"

"I was asking. What about Spesk's two deadly weapons? Did you find them?"

"Of course. You asked me to, didn't you?"

"Well?"

"Well what?" asked Remo.

"What are they?" Smith asked.

"You can't have them," Remo said.

"Why not?" Smith said.

"Some things just aren't for sale," Remo said. He pulled the telephone cord from the wall and collapsed back on the couch. Laughing.

the EXECUTIONER by Don Pendleton

Over 22 million copies in print!

☐	40-027-9	Executioner's War Book	$1.50
☐	40-299-6	War Against the Mafia	#1	1.50
☐	40-300-3	Death Squad	#2	1.50
☐	40-301-1	Battle Mask	#3	1.50
☐	40-302-X	Miami Massacre	#4	1.50
☐	40-303-8	Continental Contract	#5	1.50
☐	40-304-6	Assault on Soho	#6	1.50
☐	40-305-4	Nightmare in New York	#7	1.50
☐	40-306-2	Chicago Wipeout	#8	1.50
☐	40-307-0	Vegas Vendetta	#9	1.50
☐	40-308-9	Caribbean Kill	#10	1.50
☐	40-309-7	California Hit	#11	1.50
☐	40-310-0	Boston Blitz	#12	1.50
☐	40-311-9	Washington I.O.U.	#13	1.50
☐	40-312-7	San Diego Siege	#14	1.50
☐	40-313-5	Panic in Philly	#15	1.50
☐	40-314-3	Sicilian Slaughter	#16	1.50
☐	40-237-6	Jersey Guns	#17	1.50
☐	40-315-1	Texas Storm	#18	1.50
☐	40-316-X	Detroit Deathwatch	#19	1.50
☐	40-238-4	New Orleans Knockout	#20	1.50
☐	40-317-8	Firebase Seattle	#21	1.50
☐	40-318-6	Hawaiian Hellground	#22	1.50
☐	40-319-4	St. Louis Showdown	#23	1.50
☐	40-239-2	Canadian Crisis	#24	1.50
☐	40-224-4	Colorado Kill-Zone	#25	1.50
☐	40-320-8	Acapulco Rampage	#26	1.50
☐	40-321-6	Dixie Convoy	#27	1.50
☐	40-225-2	Savage Fire	#28	1.50
☐	40-240-6	Command Strike	#29	1.50
☐	40-150-7	Cleveland Pipeline	#30	1.50
☐	40-166-3	Arizona Ambush	#31	1.50
☐	40-252-X	Tennessee Smash	#32	1.50
☐	40-333-X	Monday's Mob	#33	1.50
☐	40-334-8	Terrible Tuesday	#34	1.50